MISSION SURVIVAL

TRACKS OF THE TIGER

www.**missionsurvival**.co.uk

CHARACTER PROFILES

Beck Granger

At just thirteen years old, Beck Granger knows more about the art of survival than most military experts learn in a lifetime. When he was young he travelled with his parents to some of the most remote places in the world, from Antarctica to the African Bush, and he picked up many vital survival skills from the tribes he met along the way.

Uncle Al

Professor Sir Alan Granger is one of the world's most respected anthropologists. His stint as a judge on a reality television show made him a household name, but to Beck he will always be plain old Uncle Al – more comfortable in his lab with a microscope than hob-nobbing with the rich and famous. He believes that patience is a virtue and has a 'never-say-die' attitude to life. For the past few years he has been acting as guardian to Beck, who has come to think of him as a second father.

David & Melanie Granger

Beck's mum and dad were Special Operations Directors for the environmental direct action group, Green Force. Together with Beck, they spent time with tribes in some of the world's most extreme places. Several years ago their light plane mysteriously crashed in the jungle. Their bodies were never found and the cause of the accident remains unknown . . .

Peter Grey

Beck's best friend from school may not be much to look at, but his small and slim figure belies a boy who is brave, determined and only occasionally stubborn. Having known Beck for many years, the two have a firm bond in spite of their constant bickering. He is rarely to be seen without his pride and joy – the digital camera he got for his birthday.

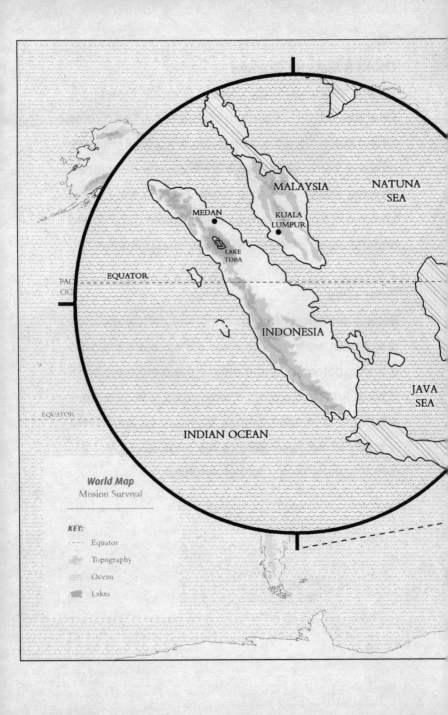

MALAYSIA

NATUNA SEA

MEDAN

KUALA LUMPUR

LAKE TOBA

EQUATOR

PAC OC

INDONESIA

JAVA SEA

EQUATOR

INDIAN OCEAN

World Map
Mission Survival

KEY:

- - - - Equator

Topography

Ocean

Lakes

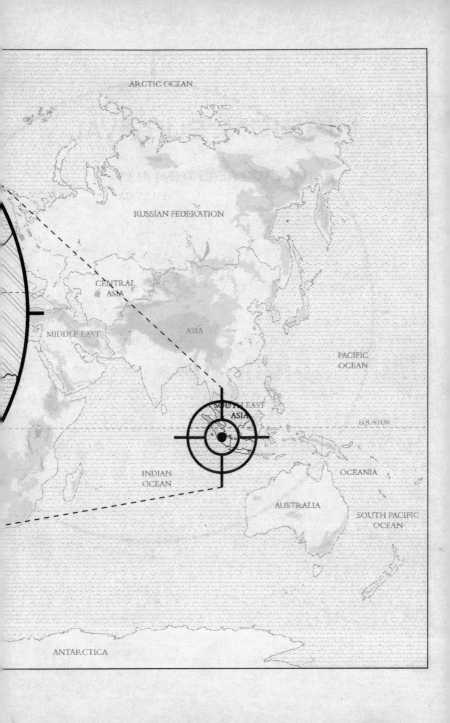

MISSION SURVIVAL

HAVE YOU READ THEM ALL?

GOLD OF THE GODS

Location: The Colombian jungle

Dangers: Snakes; starvation; howler monkeys

Beck travels to Colombia in search of the legendary City of Gold. Could a mysterious amulet provide the key to uncovering a secret that was thought to be lost for ever?

WAY OF THE WOLF

Location: The Alaskan mountains

Dangers: Snow storms; wolves; white-water rapids

After his plane crashes in the Alaskan wilderness, Beck has to stave off hunger and the cold as he treks through the frozen mountains in search of help.

SANDS OF THE SCORPION
Location: The Sahara Desert
Dangers: Diamond smugglers; heatstroke; scorpions

Beck is forced into the Sahara Desert to escape a gang of diamond smugglers. Can he survive the heat and evade the smugglers as he makes his way back to safety?

TRACKS OF THE TIGER
Location: The Indonesian wilderness
Dangers: Volcanoes; tigers; orang-utans

When a volcanic eruption strands him in the jungles of Indonesia, Beck must test his survival skills against red-hot lava, a gang of illegal loggers, and the tigers that are on his trail . . .

CLAWS OF THE CROCODILE

Location: The Australian Outback

Dangers: Flash floods; salt-water crocodiles; deadly radiation

Beck heads to the Outback in search of the truth about the plane crash that killed his parents. But somebody wants the secret to remain hidden – and they will kill to protect it.

TRACKS OF THE TIGER
A RED FOX BOOK 978 1 862 30481 9

First published in Great Britain by Red Fox
an imprint of Random House Children's Publishers UK
A Random House Group Company

First published in Red Fox, 2010
This edition published 2013

11 13 15 14 12

Copyright © Bear Grylls, 2010
Cover artwork © Paul Carpenter, 2013
Map artwork © Ben Hasler, 2013

The Random House Group Limited supports the Forest Stewardship Council® (FSC®), the
leading international forest certification organisation. Our books carrying the FSC label are
printed on FSC®-certified paper. FSC is the only forest-certification scheme supported by
the leading environmental organisations, including Greenpeace. Our paper procurement
policy can be found at www.randomhouse.co.uk/environment.

MIX
Paper from
responsible sources
FSC
www.fsc.org   FSC® C016897

Set in Swiss 721 BT

Red Fox Books are published by Random House Children's Publishers UK,
61–63 Uxbridge Road, London W5 5SA

www.**randomhousechildrens**.co.uk
www.**randomhouse**.co.uk

Addresses for companies within The Random House Group Limited can be found at:
www.randomhouse.co.uk/offices.htm

THE RANDOM HOUSE GROUP Limited Reg. No. 954009

A CIP catalogue record for this book is available from the British Library.

Printed and bound in Great Britain by CPI Group (UK) Ltd, Croydon, CR0 4YY

MISSION SURVIVAL

TRACKS
OF THE TIGER

BEAR GRYLLS

RED FOX

To my brilliant godchildren: Hubie, Scarlett,
Emmeline, George, Barnabas, Emily,
Rufus, Pip, Caspar and Alfie.
Here's to some great adventures ahead!

CHAPTER 1

The three volcanoes seemed to be moving steadily towards the rickety bus. They looked like a child's drawing – perfect cones that rose up above the Indonesian jungle for hundreds of metres. Puffs of smoke rose from the top. One was far away on the horizon, one was slightly nearer, and one was so close you had to press your face to the swaying window to see all of it.

The bus tilted as its load of tourists crowded over to one side to peer out. Beck Granger had been sitting nearest the window and he felt himself being pushed against the glass.

From the plane the jungle had looked like a sea. Its waves were the endless canopy of leaves that rose and fell with the ground beneath it. Its spray was the mists that burst out of the saturated air when it could hold no more water. Instead of fish, it was home to countless reptiles, insects and mammals. In place of sharks, crocodiles patrolled its rivers, and tigers roamed in the dark depths beneath the trees. It stretched as far as the eye could see and covered most of the island of Sumatra.

Now they were down in the jungle's heart. It was right outside the windows, rattling past at thirty miles an hour. A tangled mass of hundreds of square miles of virgin rainforest. And within it, thousands of different plant species all scrabbled for growing space. Each plant had only one objective, and that was to be slightly higher than the others so that it could reach the sky and soak up the sun's rays. The searing heat and the humidity meant that they had all the energy and water they needed. Now all they had to do was grow.

The volcanoes had been hidden by the tangle of trees and undergrowth that crowded in on either side of the bumpy road. Then the bus drove through this clearing and they just appeared. The nearest was so close you couldn't tell it was a volcano – it just looked like another mountain, until you looked more closely. The steep sides were covered in thick vegetation but wisps of smoke rose from hidden clefts in the rock. It looked like the kind of place dragons might be hiding. Beck smiled to himself at the thought, but then the smile faded.

He had visited this part of the world before. For a while he had lived with his parents in a village in Borneo. The native people had taught him how to survive in the jungle, how to live with the land rather than against it, how to find food and water and, most importantly, how to look after himself. But he had never been near an active volcano. That was something he didn't know about, but he had naturally been intrigued.

Beck knew that if you were properly prepared, there was no reason you couldn't survive . . . well, anywhere, really. But he also knew that if a volcano exploded in the wrong place, you were dead – end of story. Volcanoes were a force that humankind couldn't control and probably never would. They looked magnificent from a distance, but Beck was quietly glad that this was as close as they were going to get.

Behind him, someone breathed in awe. 'Good grief.' Mr Grey, his friend Peter's dad, was looking out of the window over Beck's shoulder. 'What a sight.'

'Dad, we've been up Vesuvius.' That was Peter in the seat beside Beck, practical and matter-of-fact.

'Yes, but you don't normally expect to be able to see three volcanoes together without even moving your head.'

The tour guide was saying much the same thing to the rest of the bus. He was a small, wiry Malay man with a big grin. The tourists listened avidly as he told them that a line of volcanic activity, known as the 'Ring of Fire', ran all around the Pacific Rim. It started in New Zealand, then ran up past Australia, through Southeast Asia, past Japan and China, then round and down past the west coasts of North and South America. Indonesia sat smack on the Ring and had over a hundred active volcanoes. Its collection included possibly the most famous of the lot, Krakatoa.

The guide continued, 'Now, this gentleman on our left' – he indicated the closest of the volcanoes – 'would be Mount Lasa. He's quite safe – hasn't erupted at all recently. The Lasa National Park, where we are now, is named after him and he looks after us all. We will be passing around the base of the volcano and will arrive at the sanctuary in about an hour . . .'

Peter and his father sat down again. Beck settled back in his seat and closed his eyes. They had got up early to catch the bus. He would rest for the next hour, while the bus carried them away from the volcano and towards what he was really looking forward to.

CHAPTER 2

'*Bohongit!*'

'Bless you, Dad,' Peter said.

'Ha, ha.' Mr Grey was an older, taller version of Peter. Same fair hair (but receding), same lanky build, same glasses. It made Beck wonder if there had been a scientific breakthrough in human cloning about thirteen years ago. Mr Grey tapped the map. 'I mean, the Bohongit Orang-utan Sanctuary, where we're going tomorrow!'

They had been lounging by the side of the hotel pool in Medan, shaded from the equatorial sun by huge parasols. When Mr Grey sat down next to them he was wrestling with a map about the same size as him.

Peter was jiggling his baby sister, Hannah, on his

lap. They were playing a game in which he would hand her a rattle. She would take it, and shake it, and maybe put it in her mouth. Then she would lean over and drop it. When it hit the ground she would look up at her brother with wide eyes that seemed to say, *Wow, that's amazing!* And Peter would pick up the rattle and give it back to her so that the process could repeat itself. Hannah seemed certain that with enough patience she could catch gravity out.

As far as Beck was aware, none of the Grey family except Peter had ever been out of Europe before. Now they had decided to remedy that with a holiday in Indonesia. The Greys had invited him along out of the kindness of their hearts, and because Peter was his best friend at school, and because they had some strange idea that they owed Beck for their son's life.

As far as Beck was concerned, he owed just as much to Peter in return.

The Greys had thrown themselves in at the deep end with a strange mixture of enthusiasm, careful planning (activities carefully timetabled for each day) and leaving things to luck (bringing a baby on a holiday like this in the first place). Beck could see where Peter got it from.

'Where *you're* going tomorrow,' Peter's mum corrected. She had a smile for everyone and everything. Her level, calm approach to life balanced out the enthusiasms of the men in the family. Beck had once made the mistake of thinking she was a bit of a pushover, until he and Peter got back from their adventure in the Sahara. Then there had been tears of joy that her son was safe, yes, but she had also made it quite clear what she thought of the way they had got into the trouble in the first place.

They had recklessly followed some men they thought might be smugglers. Then they had recklessly managed to get trapped on a plane with them and an illegal cargo of diamonds . . . Peter's mum had told them in no uncertain terms that 'reckless' was not to happen again.

Beck now knew she ruled the family with a rod of iron that she kept carefully out of sight. They all realized it was there, and that was what counted. She had no intention of letting them get into any more trouble, and Beck had no intention of getting into any either.

'It's a long trip for a baby,' she explained. 'Hannah and I will stay here and do some exploring. Won't we, darling? Yes we will, *yes* we *will* . . .'

Hannah had cried for most of the plane journey here. In the last week Beck had learned more about babies than he'd ever thought possible, and he was pretty sure you were meant to keep them in the shade.

'Is it just us going?' Peter asked his father.

'Er, no. There's a tour organized through the hotel – what are you smiling at, Beck?'

'Nothing!' Beck assured him. 'Nothing!'

But the truth was, it had suddenly struck him how strange it was to be doing something like this with a family. He was abroad on an actual, proper holiday, and the only purpose was fun and relaxation. No conferences to go to, no tribes to study, no environmental projects to examine. It was a strange concept – not something he had done much of in his nearly fourteen years of life.

Beck would never be surrounded by his own family because his family consisted of just Uncle Al. He was currently somewhere in the Russian steppes, interviewing nomadic tribal leaders. Beck's parents had died very early in his life and they had always been too busy to produce any siblings for him. He remembered them always on the move, simultaneously working on at least two or three projects for the Green Force environmental action group.

If they were alive, if Beck had a brother or sister, would they ever have been relaxing by the pool of a tourist hotel in Indonesia? Or taking organized tours to orang-utan sanctuaries? Beck doubted it. They would have made their own private visit. They would have arranged an action plan with the locals to help preserve the orang-utans' habitat. They would have met with local politicians and worked to raise consciousness around the world.

Just go to look? Never!

Beck loved the way he had been brought up. If he'd had a normal family, he wouldn't have spent time with remote tribes in deserts and jungles around the world, and he wouldn't have learned the things he knew about staying alive in the most extreme places. On the other hand, he could have maybe done without the escaping drug smugglers in

South America, or the diamond smugglers in North Africa . . .

Beck was proud of the good work undertaken by Uncle Al and Green Force. There was nothing wrong with it. But there was also nothing to say you couldn't have a relaxing holiday too!

'We need to be up early,' Mr Grey told the two boys. 'The coach leaves at seven. And after the sanctuary, we're going on to look at some fantastic ruins left over from the Sailendra dynasty.'

'What did the Sailendra dynasty do?' asked Peter.

'No idea,' Mr Grey replied. 'Died, and left a lot of ruins . . .'

Ruins, eh? Beck thought.

CHAPTER 3

The air that gusted through the bus was jungle air. It had the taste and smell of a billion tons of vegetation. In Medan, on the coast, the air smelled of salt from the sea and petrol from the traffic. But the jungle air lurked outside the city limits, ready to pounce on you like a tiger as soon as you left.

The road was potholed. Tarmac didn't stand a chance. Plants constantly burst up out of it, pushing it aside, before being crushed to death by the traffic. The jungle was the life form that ruled this island. Beck had the feeling that even a large city like Medan could only really exist here because the jungle temporarily allowed it.

The bus was battered and dented too. Its springs had been crushed into submission a long time ago.

The only air conditioning was the open windows, so there was a good through draught – but the air wasn't cool. It was hot and sticky, and had hardly any cooling effect on your sweating body.

Every now and then the trees vanished on one side or the other and they passed through paddy fields, perfectly flat and a vivid green. Indonesian farm workers laboured here, bent double as they reached down to the ground. From a distance it looked like they were up to their knees in tall green grass. In fact, Beck knew, they were wading through muddy water. This was how rice was grown. The work was dirty and wet and back-breaking, but rice had been the staple diet for generations here.

A hand patted him on the shoulder.

'Are you sure you're not too hot, Beck?'

Mr Grey sat in the row behind them. There had been a minor clash of wills before leaving the hotel. Mr Grey's thinking was: *It's hot, like summer, so the boys should wear T-shirts and shorts*. Beck's thinking was: *It's the jungle, and I know what that's like, so I'm wearing long trousers and a long-sleeved shirt and I'm making sure Peter does too*.

The clothes he wore were lightweight and well ventilated. They were also strong enough to provide protection against thorns and insect bites and anything else the jungle could throw at them. Not that Beck was expecting anything to be thrown at them, but you never knew.

Mrs Grey had been on Beck's side. Her son was fair haired and fair skinned and never took well to bright sun. A couple of months ago, stranded in the Sahara, only Beck's quick thinking had kept him from dying of sunstroke. So she was quite happy to go with Beck's suggestion for what they should wear. Mr Grey had given in. But every ten minutes or so he still had to ask if the boys were too warm.

So Beck smiled politely again, and said, 'No, I'm fine, thanks.'

The boys exchanged glances – Beck winked and Peter grinned. At least they could all agree about hats to keep the sun off, and sensible footwear – shoes that were sturdy and tough. Everyone on the bus wore them – the tour guide had told them to. Peter's dad might have preferred them to wear sandals, but if it came from an adult in authority, then it was all right . . .

Peter pulled his camera out for a last shot of Mount Lasa before it disappeared behind the trees again. Sometimes he seemed to treat his camera like another baby sister. He had even bought it a water-tight carrying case for this trip, to protect it from the humid air.

Beck had to smile again when he saw it. That camera had got them into a whole host of trouble, back in the Sahara. It had been Peter's determination to take some good shots that had got them trapped on that aeroplane in the first place.

Peter caught his eye and brandished the camera. 'Ready for lots of pics of the monkey zoo!'

Beck laughed. 'I don't think they like being called monkeys,' he told Peter with a grin, 'and it'll be much more than a zoo . . .'

CHAPTER 4

'Look,' the guide whispered. 'Down there . . . by the rocks . . .'

Twenty tourists held their breath.

The river was shallow and rocky, flowing over a gravel bed as wide as two roads. It was a soothing sound that blended in with the jungle noise of innumerable birds and animals and insects. On either side the rainforest formed ten-metre walls of trees and bush beneath an impenetrable canopy of leaves and branches. Tangles of vines and trunks were like vertical cables. It was difficult to say what was holding the tree canopy up and what was hanging down from it.

But on the far bank, something moved. A small figure wrapped in orange-brown fur crawled out from behind the rocks at the water's edge. It looked mostly human with a bit of spider thrown in. A body the size of a small child and absurdly long arms and legs. The orang-utan had been washing itself in the shallows at the edge of the water.

The tourists let out their breaths again with a collective 'Aaah . . .'

There was a whirring by Beck's ear as Peter zoomed in with his camera.

'She's got a baby!' Peter said in delight. 'Look!'

He passed the camera to Beck so that his friend could see it in close-up. He had already noticed the much smaller orange lump clinging to its mother's back. She loped on all fours up the bank, away from the river and the watching humans.

'Hey! Monkey! Over here!' one of the tourists called. The reverent atmosphere burst like a balloon. The orang-utan paused and looked back at them. Her face was long and grave, as if wondering how anyone could be such an idiot. Then she turned away again and disappeared into the trees.

'Hah!' The man clapped his hands, very pleased with himself. Then: 'What?' as he noticed the expressions on some of the faces around him. 'I made her look, didn't I? We travel for three hours in a hot bus, you want to see something at the other end!'

Beck gave Peter a nudge. 'Yeah, but do *they* want to see *you*?'

Peter grinned.

Their guide was a middle-aged Malay man called Nakula. His keeper's uniform made him look a bit like an overgrown schoolboy. His face was lined and inscrutable, but as he had met the tourists getting off the bus, Beck reckoned he saw a flash of utter dislike. Beck could understand that. If you worked as a keeper in an orang-utan sanctuary, presumably you would want to spend your time keeping orang-utans, not looking after rich western tourists. Unfortunately, though, that was how the sanctuary actually made the money to care for orang-utans in the first place . . .

This particular tourist really wasn't doing anything to improve the reputation of westerners.

'The orang-utans are fed twice a day, sir,' Nakula said with icy politeness. 'That will be your best chance of seeing them up close. Now, if you would like to come along . . .'

'It's like we're guests in their home, isn't it?' Peter said to his dad as they followed after Nakula. 'We're the ones who should be living up to expectations, not them.'

At the back of the group the loud tourist was explaining to anyone who would listen why he thought the whole trip was a rip-off. Peter shook his head angrily. Nakula noticed Peter and Beck's annoyance, and for a moment it looked like he might be prepared to dislike these two tourists a little less than everyone else.

'They are very solitary, private creatures,' he explained, for the benefit of the group. 'And why should they not be? This is their home' – he half nodded to Peter in acknowledgement, and Peter flushed a little, as if he had been praised – 'and humans spoil it.'

'Pollution?' someone asked.

'Loggers,' Nakula answered. The loathing in his voice made it sound like a swear word, something you wouldn't use to describe your worst enemy. 'The wood of our rainforest is in demand in your west. The orang-utans live in trees. The trees are cut down – where can they go? They die. How easy would it be for us all to survive if the orang-utans started to knock down our houses?'

'But they're protected here,' a woman pointed out.

'They are protected *here*, but those in the wild are not. Fewer and fewer survive each year.'

They walked on through the jungle. Beck was pleased to see that the sanctuary made a minimal impact on the environment. The paths were artificial, packed with gravel and woodchip, but otherwise it was just pure jungle around them: hot, humid and heaving with life. It was a couple of years since he'd last visited a jungle properly. He enjoyed renewing the acquaintance.

Every now and then the shadowy form of an orang-utan swung through the trees around them, but they were surprisingly hard to see. You assumed that their colour would stand out a mile, but they easily blended into the shades and shadows of the treetops. You heard them more than anything else.

Branches crackled and leaves rustled, and you got the briefest glimpse of a vaguely human shape gliding effortlessly through the canopy. Peter tried to take a couple of pictures but they moved too fast.

He tugged on Beck's elbow. 'Do you think it's safe to leave the path?'

Beck shook his head, smiling. 'Leaving the path is a *bad idea*, Peter.' His friend looked crestfallen and Beck pounced. This was too good a chance to miss to wind Peter up. 'There's tigers lurking behind every tree just waiting to bite your head off the moment you stray off it,' he said dramatically. 'That's if the poisonous snakes and insects don't get you first. Oh, and that's not to mention the man-eating plants . . .'

By now Peter had guessed it was a wind-up. He tilted his head and looked sceptically at Beck.

'Of course you can leave the path,' Beck told him. 'Why?'

'I just want to take a picture.'

There was a cluster of bright red flowers a couple of metres away. They were enormous, the size of plates, and gave off a sickly smell that had already lured several insects to their death. Peter stepped off the path and zoomed in close with the lens.

'I suppose there really are tigers and things in the jungle, though?' he asked, not looking up from his camera.

'Well, yeah. But they won't come near the inhabited areas unless they're desperate.'

Beck used the opportunity to take a swig of water from the bottle in his backpack. He had politely turned down the offer of a soft drink for the trip from Peter's mum. Beck knew that if you wanted to stay hydrated you couldn't beat plain water. That was the real thing. Especially in a climate as humid as the jungle.

Peter had finished taking pictures. He straightened up, turned and almost fell over. 'What the—?'

He had managed to get his foot caught in a loop of vine. He instinctively gave it a tug to free it and nearly fell over again. Another, slightly harder tug had even less success. If anything the vine grew tighter.

'Don't fight it, Peter,' Beck told him. 'You have to ease yourself free.' He took the camera so that his friend could bend down and free his foot with his hands. 'Remember, in the jungle every single plant wants to climb, so they're strong and tough and most of them have thorns or hooks or suckers . . .'

'I get the message,' Peter muttered as he straightened up for the second time, this time with two free feet. 'Don't wrestle with jungle plants because they will win.' He took his camera back.

'Yup!' Beck agreed. 'I got taught that in Borneo, when Mum and Dad were there with Green Force—'

'Green Force?' Nakula had been waiting to see there were no stragglers in the group. He hadn't been listening in, but those two words had obviously stood out in the conversation. For the first time his cool politeness was punctured by active interest. 'You were with Green Force?'

'Mum and Dad were,' Beck answered, a little taken aback by the sudden enthusiasm. In fact, their trip to Borneo had been their last trip together as a family, before the plane crash . . .

Nakula explained, 'Poachers worked near my village when I was younger. We all knew who they were, but a corrupt police chief refused to charge them. Green Force gave us funds so that we could bring our own private prosecution in the courts.'

Beck felt uncomfortable under the burning approval in the man's eyes. 'Glad they helped,' he said awkwardly.

'Your parents must have been good people,' Nakula commented.

'Well . . . yeah. I always thought so. They kind of grew on me, I guess.' Beck smiled.

Nakula laughed, and it transformed his face, making him look suddenly warm and friendly. But then the other tourists gathered round to see what was keeping them, and the professional reserve came back.

'It is almost feeding time,' he announced. 'This way . . .'

CHAPTER 5

The feeding platform for the orang-utans was in a clearing. A few manmade objects stood out – climbing frames, ropes, a cluster of huts around the edge that blended into the surroundings. Otherwise, like the rest of the sanctuary, it was kept as natural as possible.

And here there were enough orang-utans to keep even the loud tourist happy. They knew what time of day it was and they swarmed around the keepers. Small ones, large ones, baby ones with their parents. Beck could count eight, maybe ten, without even moving his head.

He remembered the one by the river, thinking it looked part human, part spider. Up close the resemblance was even stronger. The body was short and stocky with a pronounced pot belly, but the arms looked like they had been grafted on from a completely different species. They were twice as long as the legs and seemed to have a life of their own.

When an orang-utan waddled along on two legs, it had to hold its arms up to stop them dragging on the ground, as if it was wading through invisible water. Their hands were also huge – two massive leathery mitts that looked like hairy wicket keeper's gloves.

Their faces were hairless, like wrinkled leather. Beck was struck by the variety of expressions. Orang-utans could laugh – they bared their teeth and their shoulders shook. They could look thoughtful, or happy, or even angry if another orang-utan said or did something that they objected to.

When they squatted down, shoulders hunched, they suddenly looked incredibly old. They were so *almost* human. Beck could see that this was how humans might have turned out if evolution had just developed in a slightly different way. Their eyes, though, were almost always sad. They seemed to contain the wisdom of the universe, as if they knew what a mess their close relatives the humans were making of their jungle – a jungle where they themselves were totally at home.

Beck squatted down in front of a teenage orangutan which was tucking into a banana. It glanced up at him and their eyes met for a moment. Beck could have sworn he could read its thoughts: *Listen, mate, you humans need to do a lot better. Now excuse me, this banana's more interesting than you are.*

A keeper handed a bucket to an old, grizzled male, who held the handle in his teeth and trotted on all fours over to a couple of his friends. He sat in front of the bucket, then reached into it for the food. One of the others clung to a branch with one foot and one hand, and dipped his spare hand into the bucket for the food. The third hung upside down by his feet and reached into the bucket from above.

Peter was laughing so much he had trouble taking a photo. 'What do they eat?' he asked.

Nakula was standing and watching the same scene, hands in his pockets and a fond smile on his face. 'In the wild, fruit – all kinds. Here we give them only bananas and milk. We try to keep their diet boring to encourage them to forage for themselves.'

'They don't look very bored.'

'I know.' Nakula sighed. 'Perhaps we treat them too well. I would like them not to need us at all – to live freely in the jungle, in no danger from the hand of man, only visiting us when they wanted to. But at the same time, I am pleased they want to stay here because I would miss them so much if they left.'

'So, if they weren't hanging around here, where would they be?'

'Oh, they like to live on their own. At night they sleep in nests—'

'*Nests?*'

'Certainly.' Nakula laughed at Peter's surprise. 'See, up there?'

He led the boys over to the edge of the clearing and pointed up at one of the trees. Peter zoomed his camera in on the nest. It really did look like a giant bird had made it. Branches and leaves and sticks were jammed together in a fork of the tree's limbs, ten metres up.

'They rarely spend more than two nights in the

same place. They might move into a vacant nest, or make a new one just for one night. They are very – what is your word? – easygoing? And see how there is fruit nearby?' He pointed at clusters of berries that dangled above the nest. 'They like to laze around in their nests and have their food dangling at arm's length. *Very* easygoing.'

Nakula cocked his head to one side and looked thoughtfully at the two boys. It looked like he was weighing up a difficult decision.

'You two are the only young people in your group, yes? I think I know another young person who would very much like to meet you. Over here . . .'

CHAPTER 6

Nakula led them over to a hut. Beck turned and saw that Peter's father was the other side of the clearing, talking to a couple of Americans; he waved at him to let him know where they were.

Inside the hut another keeper sat on a chair with his back to them. The angle he was sitting at suggested he was feeding a baby with a bottle. When Nakula said his name, he looked up and the boys saw it was indeed a baby on his lap – a baby orang-utan.

The two men chatted briefly in Malay, and then the second keeper stood up and handed the baby over to Nakula. He smiled at the boys and left.

'This is Ayesha,' Nakula explained as he cradled the tiny orang-utan. 'She was found near her mother's dead body, too frightened to move on and find food. She almost starved to death, but we were able to save her . . .'

He grinned at the boys, guessing the answer to the question he was about to ask. 'Would you like to hold her?'

Beck got to feed her first so that Peter could take pictures. He couldn't help comparing her to baby Hannah back at the hotel. They were about the same size and weight – which meant surprisingly heavy – but Hannah wasn't a solid lump of muscle covered in soft, silky hair. Holding Ayesha was like holding a solid rubber ball. The first time Beck was given Hannah he had been terrified of hurting her. If he accidentally dropped Ayesha he was sure she would bounce straight back up again.

Hannah could wrap five fingers around one of Beck's; Ayesha's hand was large enough to engulf his own. Hannah smelled of baby lotion, but Ayesha had a pleasantly warm, musky animal odour, like a well-groomed cat. Again Beck looked into an orang-utan's eyes, and this time there was no doubting her expression. That same world-weary sadness mixed with one hundred per cent trust. *You'll look after me, won't you? You'll make sure I'm all right.*

'Course I will,' he whispered. 'Course I will . . .'

'You in here, boys?' Mr Grey poked his head round the door. 'The bus leaves in five— Ah, you've made a friend!'

'We've got to leave?' Peter sounded sad. 'We're only just starting . . .'

Nakula's face was once again blank and impassive, like when he had been talking to the loud tourist. Beck guessed that meant the less time spent with tourists, the better. In their short time in the hut, though, they had seen a very different side to Nakula. He was a man who loved the orang-utans, and he had sensed similar feelings in Beck and Peter. He'd enjoyed passing on what he knew. Suddenly he was back to his dour old self.

'Well, there are the ruins to look at—' Mr Grey pointed out.

'Very old ruins?' Beck asked.

'Oh, yes, a thousand years or more . . .'

'So it's not like they're going anywhere, is it?' Peter interrupted with a grin.

'No,' Mr Grey said patiently, 'but we are, in five minutes.'

'You are returning to Medan, sir?' Nakula asked unexpectedly.

'Well, yes, after the ruins. Why?'

'Oh . . .' Nakula shrugged. His voice had the kind of casual tone you only hear when someone has a definite plan. 'I drive there this evening. I am very happy to look after your boys and bring them back then. You see' – he indicated to Ayesha, who was still playing with her bottle in Beck's arms – 'once a baby has started feeding it is hard to interrupt.' The little orang-utan's teeth gripped the bottle tightly and sucked frantically.

'You can say that again!' said Beck, laughing.

'That's certainly true,' Peter's dad muttered, thinking of Hannah's howls if she was deprived of her bottle. 'That would be kind of you.' And to the boys: 'Am I maybe detecting that thousand-year-old classical ruins aren't totally your thing?'

'Compared to a brand-new baby orang-utan . . . ?' Peter said thoughtfully. 'Not really.'

Mr Grey sighed. He looked at the boys, looked at

Ayesha, looked at Nakula, looked at his watch. Finally he seemed to accept that this was one battle he couldn't win.

'I guess it's a wonderful chance to see this sort of work – but behave yourselves, OK?' he told the boys.

'You got it,' they replied excitedly.

Then to Nakula:

'So, what time can we expect you this evening . . . ?'

CHAPTER 7

'What happened to Ayesha's mother?' Beck shouted over the noise of the engine. He clutched at the open-topped jeep's roll bar as it lurched out of a particularly deep rut on the jungle road. The boys sat in the back, leaning forward so they could speak to Nakula as he drove.

'Did something get her?' Peter asked.

'I think she starved to death, as Ayesha would have done,' Nakula said with blunt sadness. He didn't look round, preferring to concentrate on the potholed road ahead.

They had stayed another three hours at the sanctuary, playing with Ayesha and meeting some of the other keepers and orang-utans. Each keeper had his own favourite and the boys got acquainted with them all.

Beck had never realized how individual the animals were. Each one was just as much a character as a human. They had their likes and dislikes, their own sense of humour, their own moods and tempers. It didn't matter that none of them could talk. They had ways of letting you know what they were thinking. And when, sadly, it was time for Nakula to keep his promise and drive the boys back to Medan, Beck was sure the orang-utans were sorry to see them go – Ayesha in particular.

Peter handed her over as if she was his own baby sister. She clung to her keeper's chest and watched them leave with sad coos and chirrups, and then buried her face in the man's shirt.

'Starved?' Beck asked, surprised by what Nakula had said. He knew all too well that the jungle held many deadly surprises, but starvation shouldn't be one of them. Especially not for an animal in its natural environment.

Nakula slowed to negotiate a pothole before he answered. Beck looked around. They had been driving for one hour of the three-hour journey and occasionally he recognized a landmark from their trip out that morning. The most recognizable one of all was Mount Lasa. When the road headed straight towards it, you could see the volcano looming large ahead, but mostly the trees hid it from view.

Beck worked out from the direction they'd taken that morning that they would now be heading north, straight towards the volcano, before skirting its base and carrying on eastwards back to town.

'She would have had a few favourite trees as her territory,' Nakula told him. 'If the loggers took them, then she was homeless. No other female would let her into their territory, so . . .' He shrugged. 'In the cities, the homeless can line the streets and beg. Here, no streets. They starve quickly.'

'How bad is it?' Peter called. 'The logging? You said the timber was in demand in the west.'

'Oh, yes, very much. Hardwood in particular. It is sold through Malaysia and Singapore and sent on to Europe, to the United States, to Japan . . . It has many uses – furniture, picture frames, ornaments. It brings a lot of money, which is why it always springs up again, despite what the authorities may do to stop it.'

'There's no sustainable way of doing it?'

'Oh, of course there is. There are schemes, but sustainable wood costs more. Two thirds of the logging in Indonesia is still the illegal kind. It destroys hundreds of square miles, it wipes out ecosystems . . . and there is a human cost too. If the jungle dies, then the environment dies around it. The ground erodes and water flows in different ways. The paddy fields do not flood, the crops cannot be harvested. So communities can starve too. The only people who benefit are the ones doing the illegal logging. It takes a lot of money to buy an easy conscience, but they have a lot of money—'

The jeep swerved suddenly. Beck was flung against the side of the car and had to grab hold of the bar.

'Whoa!' Peter had been jolted so hard his glasses were askew. He pushed them back onto his nose. 'Did we hit something?'

'I don't think so,' Nakula said grimly. He slowly brought the jeep to a halt. They sat with the engine ticking over, apparently waiting for something. Then the keeper jumped down from the vehicle and took a few paces along the road. It looked like he was picking his way with great care. He seemed to be testing the ground with the soles of his feet.

'What—?' Peter asked, and suddenly the whole car shook. Nakula staggered and almost fell. The trees on either side shuddered as if a mighty wave was passing through them. The usual jungle background noise of cheeps and chirps erupted into screams of protest from a million birds.

'What's happening?' Peter shouted over the racket.

'Feels like an earthquake,' Beck yelled back.

'A tremor,' Nakula corrected him. 'A big one but not serious. This close to the volcano it is not unusual. Still, it would be best to get out of here.' He pulled himself into the driver's seat and revved the engine hard. The jeep shot forward. 'Medan is well away from the volcanic area.'

Beck remembered what the tour guide had said about Indonesia and the Ring of Fire, and wondered if *anywhere* in the country was well away from volcanic activity. But he saw what Nakula meant. Right now they were practically on the flanks of a big volcano. Anywhere else would probably be safer at the moment.

BOOM!

The explosion felt like red-hot needles stabbing into their eardrums without warning. Beck and Peter both cried out and clapped their hands to their ears. The jeep swerved again but Nakula fought to control the steering wheel. He glanced back at the boys and Beck saw his lips move. He couldn't make out the words over the ringing in his ears.

The ringing slowly died away and Nakula's voice faded in, like someone turning up the volume control.

'. . . more than just tremors. It may be an eruption.'

The jeep shot through a cleared patch of jungle, and just for a moment Beck had a glimpse of Lasa, towering over the trees. A thick column of solid black smoke belched up from the summit. It was already twice the height of the volcano. Then the trees hid it from view again.

'Shouldn't there be warnings?' Peter asked.

'Sometimes. Not always. It goes off every few years – always small explosions; nothing to worry about if you are a safe distance away. It is the volcanoes that sleep for centuries that cause real destruction.'

Nakula was driving much faster now, trying to find the happy compromise between getting as far away as possible and keeping control of the jeep. A puncture could trap them here. Peter opened his mouth to say something else, but Beck just put a finger to his lips and shook his head. Nakula needed to concentrate on the driving. There was nothing either of them could do to help except sit back and let him focus.

More bangs, more hidden rumblings. Beck wasn't sure if he was pleased or sorry that the volcano was hidden from sight. If an inescapable wave of molten lava was flowing his way right now, did he want to know?

But Nakula glanced round at them and smiled. A little. 'I think we are leaving it behind,' he said. There hadn't been any more tremors now for a couple of minutes, and the bangs were getting quieter.

'Look out!' Peter shouted suddenly. Nakula turned back, but too late.

There was high ground to the left side of the road,

low on the right. Glowing red lava had poured down from the left and carved a trench across the road. It was about two metres across and they could feel the heat beating at their faces through the open window. The sides of the trench were scorched black.

Nakula was going too fast to stop. He did the only thing he could, which was turn the wheel hard. The vehicle swerved off the road and plunged down a sharp bank into the trees.

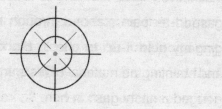

CHAPTER 8

A branch punched through the windscreen and shattered it into a thousand pieces. Beck just had time to raise an arm and ward it off, but he felt a searing pain from his elbow up to his shoulder. Then he had a confused image of green leaves rushing towards him. He and Peter bent over double as trees and branches lashed past. Their ears were assaulted by a deafening barrage of torn metal and breaking wood. Finally the jeep crashed into a tree with a thud and stopped. Peter and Beck were flung forward and their seat belts tightened into a steel grip. Then the world was still again. Beck and Peter sat there for a moment, dazed. Their ears were ringing and there was a smell of petrol in the air.

Leaves clung to Beck's head and upper body. He

instinctively lifted his hand to brush them away, and gasped as pain stabbed through his right arm. He gingerly held it up to check. Blood was welling up and staining the material of his shirt. The branch had gouged a nasty gash in him.

'Pete? You OK?'

Peter stared at him vacantly, but he was sitting up, and he didn't seem to be bleeding from any- where.

'Nakula? Uh . . . Nakula . . . ?'

Nakula was slumped forward over the steering wheel, not moving. Red, sticky blood plastered one side of his head. Something had caught him a very nasty crack. Beck gingerly released his seat belt, steeled himself and leaned forward, wincing again as his arm reminded him of the gash. He felt gently for the keeper's neck, putting his index and middle finger next to Nakula's Adam's apple. If there was a pulse, that was one place it would show, where the carotid artery beat next to the windpipe.

But there was nothing, and Beck knew with a sinking, hollow feeling that Nakula was dead.

He had a sudden flashback to the plane crash in

Alaska a few months earlier. A very similar situation, in fact. Pilot killed outright, friend Tikaani possibly injured . . . Beck felt a surge of adrenalin shoot round his body, bringing with it an urge to survive.

As a wise man once said, let the dead bury the dead. That had been his first-aid instructor's harsh, uncompromising advice, back in his cadet days. *Your first priority is to the living.*

And that meant Peter.

The smell of petrol was very strong indeed. Beck had an uncomfortable vision of it trickling onto a hot piece of metal and the jeep turning into a fireball. He jabbed at Peter's seat belt, grabbed both their day-sacks and kicked open the passenger door.

'C'mon, we're leaving.'

Peter had to be half dragged out of the jeep, but they staggered a safe distance away and collapsed at the base of a giant clump of vine-shrouded bamboo. Peter could clearly walk OK, so Beck guessed nothing was broken. Possible concussion was another matter. His friend was blinking, showing a bit more awareness than before, but he still seemed dazed.

There were four tests for concussion. Beck had used them on Tikaani that time in Alaska. Confusion, Concentration, Neurological and . . . what was the last one? Oh, yes, Memory . . . Beck smiled at the irony. Time to get to work.

'Pete . . . Pete?' Peter's gaze swam around a little but eventually it settled on Beck. 'What's your name?'

Peter sighed. 'Peter William Grey. That's the Confusion test, right? I can also do this' – he shut his eyes and touched his nose with both hands, one at a time; that was the Neurological test – 'and I can count the months of the year backwards. December, November, October, September, August—'

'OK, OK.' Beck grinned, relieved. 'You're not concussed. Though I haven't done the Memory test yet.'

'Memory test? I remember you telling me all about how you had to do this test on Tikaani. Does that count?'

'Yeah, it counts. Let's get out of here.'

'You're, uh, hurt . . .'

Peter was looking at his arm. Beck studied it again, more carefully this time. The flow of blood seemed to be slowing down. The material of his shirt was sticking to the wound and helping the blood to clot. It wasn't an ideal bandage but it was better than nothing.

'Yeah, I am.'

Then Peter went white. His gaze was fixed on Nakula. 'What about . . . ? Is he . . . ?'

'He's dead,' Beck said gently. 'There's nothing we can do.'

'I . . . I've never seen a . . .'

Most of you will never have seen a dead body before. Beck's instructor's voice was back. The man had been frank and unsympathetic but Beck had always been glad of the training. *If you ever do, you will find they all have one very distinct characteristic. They are* dead, *and that means, except in very bad movies, that they're not going anywhere.*

There was a cracking sound through the trees and Beck remembered how they had got into this in the first place. They had swerved to avoid a stream of lava. The lava was on the move.

It came flowing very slowly down the bank towards them. It didn't look immediately life-threatening, but it ate up the ground remorselessly and there was no stopping it – glowing red sludge, four metres wide and half a metre deep. The front end was charred black, and a dark crust floated on top of it. The red shone out through cracks in the crust. Whenever a leaf or a branch was touched by the flow, it flared up into flame and was consumed in seconds.

The jungle air was hot and humid. Beck could already feel a sheen of sweat clinging to his body. But the lava radiated a hot, dry heat, like an electric fire turned up way too high. If the jungle hadn't been so damp, Beck guessed it could have started a fire that would have killed them already.

He suddenly remembered the petrol. They probably had only minutes left to escape. 'We really need to get out of here,' he said.

Peter visibly pulled himself together. 'Yeah, we do.'

CHAPTER 9

Beck and Peter scrambled to their feet and looked at the jeep.

It clearly wasn't going anywhere, the wheels twisted and the engine smoking. So, Beck thought, they were on foot in the middle of the jungle . . .

His mind ran through what they had brought with them. They were dressed in reasonably good clothes for the jungle. They had bottles of water in their packs. He felt for the comforting weight at his neck, where his fire steel hung. It was a useful gadget for making fire and he (almost) never went anywhere without it.

On the other hand, they didn't have a knife, they didn't have supplies of food, they didn't have any wire or rope . . . Beck bit his lip. Peter's parents might have raised an eyebrow if he'd said he wanted to take some rope with him on the trip – but he should have brought along his pocket knife, at least.

He leaned into the back of the jeep and rummaged around with his one good hand.

'What are you doing?'

'Looking for stuff . . . anything we can use . . .'

'Like on the plane?'

'Like on the plane.'

Peter meant the plane they had been forced to jump out of over the Sahara to escape diamond smugglers who wanted to shoot them. They had searched the cargo area for anything that might help them stay alive in the desert. There had been a first aid kit, some water bottles, a knife and food. This time . . .

'There's nothing here!' Beck exclaimed in disbelief. 'Not even a first aid kit! Who goes driving in the jungle without a first aid kit?'

Beck was frantically looking under the seats, then in the side door pockets. He soon found an oil-stained roll of canvas wrapped around the jeep's wheel-changing tools. They came tumbling out onto the ground. He couldn't see a use for most of the items, but at least there was a crowbar. One end had the solid grip that fastened onto the wheel nuts. The other end was a flat wedge, like a giant screwdriver. Now, that had to be useful.

One thing there wasn't, though, was a knife. Beck couldn't imagine getting by in the jungle without one. On the other hand, fragments of the windscreen lay all around. One in particular caught his attention. It was almost fifteen centimetres long – a thin, jagged triangle that came to a very sharp point. He carefully picked it up between two fingers, holding it firmly on its flat sides. This was probably the closest he was going to get to a knife.

He leaned into the back of the jeep where they had been sitting, and pressed the tip of the glass into the seat leather. It easily punctured the covering. Beck worked it back and forth and the seat's stuffing burst out of the cut. It was dry and yellow and fluffy.

Peter was looking really anxious. 'Um, the lava's still getting closer . . . What are you doing?'

'I'm making a knife. You gather up as much

stuffing as you can and put it in our packs. It will act as tinder later on,' Beck explained.

Heat from the lava burned into his back and he blinked trickles of sweat from his eyes. He had to work quickly.

He had now cut off a strip of the leather. He needed two hands for the next bit of the job, which meant using his right hand – and that hurt. But he managed to wrap the leather round and round one end of the glass shard, and tie it off. There was still half the shard's length sticking out. Now he could grip it properly, like a knife, without slicing his hand open.

Unfortunately he didn't have any safe way of carrying it – not without breaking it or giving himself a nasty cut. He opened up one of the pockets of his daysack and dropped it in.

'The lava's getting *really* close,' Peter pointed out. He had crammed as much stuffing as he could get into both the packs.

'Right.' Beck could feel it without turning round. The front edge of the lava was maybe two metres away now. He took one last look around, but there really didn't seem to be anything more they could use. They had daysacks, with water bottles and a lot of seat stuffing. They had a knife, of sorts. They had the crowbar. And that was it.

And then he gave Nakula a final check. The force of the crash had pushed the wheel and the dashboard right back against the driver. Nakula's body was pinned in the wreckage. They could probably get him free, but it would be a lot more complicated than just undoing his seat belt. It would take time that they didn't have.

I'm sorry, he thought.

The air around him was shimmering with heat. A cluster of bushes right next to him suddenly burst into flame and Beck staggered backwards. Peter just managed to prevent him from falling.

Beck picked up his daysack and swung it onto his back. He look around and saw what looked like an animal trail leading away from the crash site. It was a line of slightly less densely packed vegetation, anyway. It was as good a way to go as any.

'Come on,' he said.

The lava reached the wrecked jeep before Beck

and Peter had even gone another ten metres. There was a high-pitched whine and then a violent explosion. A blast of burning air slammed into their backs and knocked them to the ground – though the mass of vegetation absorbed most of the impact. As Beck and Peter picked themselves up, they saw orange flames flickering through the trees and heard the crackling of burning wood and smelled scorched rubber.

Beck sent up a final silent prayer for the soul of Nakula. He wondered what religion the keeper had been. Indonesia was officially Muslim but had a strong Hindu past. He was pretty certain Muslims preferred to bury their dead. Hindus went in for cremation, didn't they? In that case he hoped Nakula was a Hindu. But whatever the man had been, he would surely have understood why they had to leave him. Beck prayed to the God he knew; he prayed silently and quickly – for Nakula, and for the strength to survive themselves.

'So, now what?' Peter asked quietly.

'I don't know. Let me think.'

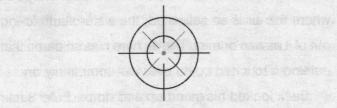

CHAPTER 10

Beck took in their surroundings. He couldn't see the lava but it might still be coming. Hopefully it would cool down before it got much further. A burning smell still forced its way through the damp leaves, and there was the small matter of an enormous exploding volcano a short distance away. They needed to check how that was doing.

The animal trail they had been following had just vanished, dissolving into the foliage – a common experience in the jungle. Dead leaves and vines were thick beneath their feet. Above them the canopy made it as gloomy as an overcast day – they couldn't see the sun or the sky. The surrounding trees and vines trapped the heat and the moisture of the jungle. It would be at least seventy or eighty per cent humidity – one hundred per cent being the point where the air is so saturated, the water starts falling out of it as rain or mist. The air here was so damp that nothing it touched could ever feel completely dry.

Beck looked his friend up and down. Peter's hair was matted and his clothes clung to his body. Beck knew he didn't look any better – probably worse, in fact, thanks to the cut in his arm. They were both sweating, but in this humidity the sweat wouldn't be able to evaporate and would therefore have no cooling effect. And the wound to his arm was only going to get worse.

Jungles are like that: everything grows bigger and faster in the jungle, and that includes bacteria. An open wound could go septic very quickly indeed. If gangrene set in, as cells of his body died and rotted, his arm could need amputating just to save his life.

'We've got to get back to civilization,' Beck said. 'End of.' He looked up at the canopy above them. 'But first we need to— *Arghh!* '

He had reached up with his right hand to wipe the sweat from his eyes. The cut in his arm had died down to a dull throb, but the movement made it spark with pain again.

'You need to bandage that,' Peter said decisively. He swung his pack off his back and started to rummage around in it, carefully pushing the seat stuffing to one side.

'There wasn't a first aid kit,' Beck muttered sourly, but he knew Peter was right. Even if he couldn't bandage it, he could clean it up. He started to look around for anything he could use. Peter's triumphant 'Ta-da!' made him turn back.

Peter had produced a clean T-shirt from his pack. 'Mum always packs me a spare,' he explained. 'Will this do?'

Beck's face creased into a grin. 'She fusses, but she knows her stuff!' he replied. 'I can cut it up and make several bandages out of it . . .' He glanced quickly at the shirt's owner. 'If that's all right with you?'

Peter shrugged. 'Be my guest. It's only an old school one. If it was my favourite Marmaduke Duke T-shirt then you'd just have to bleed.'

'I didn't know you liked Marmaduke Duke.'

'It's a recent thing!' Peter added wryly.

'OK.' Beck laughed. 'Anyway, first up I need to put some disinfectant on the cut.'

'You said there wasn't a first aid kit.'

'There wasn't' – Beck had seen what he needed – 'but there is this!'

Every tree in sight was draped with vines. They snaked their way through and around the trunks and interwove with other vines. Beck was after one in particular. Its stem was thick, three or four centimetres, and its leaves were thin and spiky.

'This is rattan,' Beck explained. He poked about through the leaves – gingerly in case he disturbed something with teeth or a stinger that didn't want to be disturbed. 'It looks like a vine, but it's actually a palm that *thinks* it's a vine. It has about a hundred and one different uses, and one of them . . . . Hah!'

Beck had found a cluster of rusty brown-red berries that clung to a stalk sprouting from the vine. 'And one of them,' he repeated, 'is as an antiseptic. It's used a lot in Chinese medicine.'

He picked five or six of the berries, held them in the palm of his hand and pressed his hands together.

He felt the berries split and their juices spurt against his skin. Beck rubbed his hands together to work the mangled berries into a red paste, which he wiped onto his right palm.

'Um – could you roll my sleeve up for me . . . ?'

Peter folded the sleeve up to Beck's shoulder and got his first close-up view of the wound. It was long and jagged but he was glad to see that it seemed quite clean. The skin had been torn roughly by he wasn't sure what, but there was hardly any debris or dirt in the wound. That was a good sign at least.

Beck dabbed the fingers of his left hand into the paste and cautiously wiped it onto the cut.

'*Ee-ahh!*' His breath hissed between clenched teeth. It stung like an army of ants gnawing into his flesh.

Peter opened his mouth and Beck glared at him. 'If you say anything your mum would say, like *If it's not hurting it's not working* then I'm leaving you here.'

Peter closed his mouth again.

'Now, get some water and pour it on. It'll just start to fester if I leave it in the wound.' He realized he was sounding a little curt. 'Um, please?'

Peter silently did as he was asked, pouring water up and down Beck's arm out of one of their bottles so that it washed over the wound. It streamed red with lumps of rattan fruit and clotted blood. Next Beck used the glass knife to cut off a broad strip of clean T-shirt and a couple of shorter, thinner strips. Peter wrapped the broad strip around his arm, over the cut, and used the thinner strips to tie it in place.

'How does that feel?'

'Much better. Thanks.'

It still ached like anything, but Beck felt better knowing that it was clean and covered. He let his sleeve fall down again and buttoned it up at his wrist.

'So, what do we do now?' asked Peter.

'First . . .' Beck studied the nearest tree carefully. Its trunk was sturdy, it wasn't too wide and there were enough branches to provide footholds. 'I want a look at that volcano. See what we're up against. Could you give me a hand up?'

Peter wrapped the fingers of his hands together and held them out at waist height in a stirrup. Beck put his foot into it and found that he could now reach the first of the tree's branches.

CHAPTER 11

Beck's arm ached but he seemed to be managing. He made his way up through the layers of jungle. For the first six or seven metres it was all bushes and saplings – young trees. Above them was the fruit layer. Hiding away in the confusion of leaves he saw clusters of green bananas, twenty or thirty to a bunch, and the smooth green balls of figs, among others.

This was where the branches began to get thinner and he had to take a bit more care where he put his feet. Every time he moved a foot to a new place, he checked it carefully to see if it would hold his weight. He climbed trees exactly the same way he would climb rocks or cliffs. The human body has four points of contact – two hands, two feet. Beck had always been told to keep three of those steady and only ever move one foot or one hand at a time. That way you always kept yourself supported, even if one point of contact failed.

Up and up. After the fruit was the layer of palms and ferns and bamboos, all covered with lichens and mosses. And finally there was the tree canopy. It was a solid blanket of leaves strung together by liana vines that provided natural bridges for the animal life up here. And it all took its energy from the sun, which powered the ecosystem of the rainforest. Beck emerged, blinking, into the sunlight.

He felt like a small animal poking his head out of the ground. The jungle canopy was a green plain that stretched away on all sides, a mad mixture of shapes and shades of green. He didn't have time to admire it. Mount Lasa occupied all his attention.

It was about a mile away. At this time of day – mid afternoon – Beck knew the sun would be halfway between the north and the west. The sun was behind his left shoulder and he was looking straight at Lasa, which he knew was to the north. Streaks of glowing red lava ran down its sides, but the most impressive sight was the smoke. It was a black, sulphurous, fan-shaped cloud that billowed up from the peak. It rose up and up until Beck's neck ached trying to see how high it went and he almost fell backwards out of the tree. It looked more solid than the mountain – like some hideous growth, a massive organism that had burst out of the earth.

Towards the top it leaned over, blown towards the east. Beck let out a cautious sigh of relief. Medan was to the north-east. If the smoke and ash from the volcano was heading due east, it would miss the city and Peter's family.

It still lay between them, though.

Beck took a final look around but there was no sign of civilization – no hint of the hand of man. They really were on their own. In the middle of the jungle.

Thoughtfully he started to climb back down again.

Peter was waiting for him at the base of the tree. Beck sat down next to him and reported what he had seen.

'The jungle's not on fire. That's maybe the key thing.'

'There won't be any helicopters flying while the volcano's erupting,' Peter pointed out. 'They'll miss us but they won't be able to come looking.'

'Nope. We need to go to them. So . . .' Beck thought for a minute. 'The question is, do we head back or go on? I mean, if we just went back along the road, we'd get to the sanctuary. Eventually. And walking along the road'll be a whole lot easier than getting through the jungle.'

'Yes, but the volcano will be throwing out lava and hot pumice in all directions. We want to head away from it.'

Beck grinned. 'Let me guess – you did a school project on volcanoes?'

'No, I just paid attention when we went to see Pompeii. You've heard of Pompeii?'

'Ancient Roman town buried by a volcano? OK, we go forward.'

And that, Beck thought, was a key decision. That simple little choice put them into a survival situation. Instinctively he began to run through a list in his head. The four priorities of survival – protection, rescue, water, food. Protection? First of all from the lava – that meant they had to get moving. Rescue? Not while the volcano was erupting – if they were to survive, they would need to make it happen themselves. To self-rescue. Water and food? Plenty of that around . . .

'We need to head south-east,' Peter said firmly, derailing Beck's thoughts. 'The coast is to the east, so that's where we'll find people, and west would just take us further into the jungle.'

Beck blinked in surprise. 'Absolutely,' he agreed. 'But Medan's to the north-east. Let's just skirt around the volcano. We can move faster than lava . . .'

'No.' Peter shook his head emphatically. 'We *really don't* want to go under that cloud. Not if we can avoid it. For a start, it'll be raining ash down on us. And then there's the pyroclastic flow.'

Beck felt like his friend had just lapsed into a strange new language. 'The paralytic *what*?'

'Pyroclastic flow. It's when you get this huge column of rock and ash and stuff, right, all getting blown into the air by the volcano. And because the air is so hot, superheated, it stays up. That's what you saw. And we're talking thousands, millions of tons of it. But sooner or later the volcano cools down again, and the air isn't hot enough to hold it up . . . and all that stuff comes crashing down on top of you.'

'OK . . .' Beck shifted uneasily. 'So if it happens, we take shelter—'

'No. No.' Peter was waving his hands in the air in frustration, trying to weave his words together in a way Beck would understand. 'Doesn't work. Look. Pompeii was destroyed by Vesuvius, which is five miles away. Witnesses saw the pyroclastic flow get there in about a minute, and it buried the whole town completely. That's how much there is of it, and that's how fast it travels. And did I mention – yeah, I think I did – there's thousands of tons of it – and, oh, it's about a thousand degrees . . .'

'Tell you what.' Beck held up his hand to shut off the flow of words. 'I've had a really great idea. Why don't we get out of here and head south-east, away from the volcano?'

'Wow,' Peter said admiringly. 'That's leadership! Take my idea and make it yours!'

They pushed themselves up to their feet.

'We can argue those finer points on the move.' Beck smiled in return. 'Oh – but there's one other thing you need to know . . .' he added.

'What's that?' Peter replied, all unsuspecting.

'We're also in tiger territory,' Beck said grimly, and this time he wasn't joking.

CHAPTER 12

'This,' Peter muttered, 'is blinkin' tiring.'

The sounds of the volcano were muffled behind them and the jungle was regaining its natural voice. Beck's sense of direction and the occasional glimpse of sky told him they were heading the right way.

They had paused in the green gloom of the jungle to finish off their water bottles. The best way to carry spare water was inside you. Back in the Sahara, every drop had counted and an accidental spillage had almost caused disaster. Many things might happen to them here in the jungle, but one thing that was not on the cards was dying of thirst. There was plenty of water around and Beck knew how to get it.

But Peter was struggling already. In the Sahara you could choose a direction and start walking. Even here, the jungle wasn't an impenetrable barrier as long as you approached it properly. But Peter was finding that with every step the vegetation seemed to push you back.

'Imagine you're back home in London,' Beck said. He tried to put it in terms that Peter could understand. 'Oxford Street, the last weekend before Christmas, right? What's it like?'

'The streets are totally packed,' Peter said with a shudder.

'Exactly. Crowds everywhere, blocking your way. There's no way you can walk straight from A to B. So you have to twist and turn and bend your body and shorten or lengthen your stride. You don't walk straight ahead, you slide through at all sorts of angles.'

'Oxford Street, weekend before Christmas,' Peter said ironically. He took a look around at the branches and vines that hemmed them in. 'Got it.'

'Think twice before you do anything or touch anything,' Beck added. 'One bite from the wrong creature can kill you. Even one sting can disable you, and that'll kill you in the long run.' He stomped on the ground for emphasis. 'Don't sneak about. Walk with a good heavy footfall.'

'Because of snakes?' Peter guessed.

'Because of snakes,' Beck confirmed.

'Wow, it's like being in the desert again, isn't it? Apart from, you know, all the trees and rain and animals and total lack of sand.'

Beck laughed. 'There's differences too. The snakes are less afraid of you here. They won't get out of your way so quickly. If one's on a branch that's next to you, say – well, it might not move at all. Until you accidentally reach out and touch it. Then it'll bite you.

'And here, we *do not* walk at night. Not at all.'

In the desert they had done most of their walking by night, out of the blistering heat of the sun.

'Night is when the nasties come out, and here on the equator night falls very quickly. Day and night are the same length. So . . .' Beck checked his watch. It was getting on for four in the afternoon. 'In another hour, five o'clock, we'll stop, and get some food together, and make a shelter.'

Food. The lack of supplies was another matter that was weighing on Beck's mind. When he had been thrown into a situation like this before, he had usually had a small reserve of food to start with. Not this time, though.

'So where are we walking to?' Peter asked quietly. Beck glanced sideways at him. His friend's face was set and thoughtful. Beck's stomach gave a lurch as he registered it.

They were in an environment even more hostile than the Sahara. The Sahara could have killed them with heat, thirst or starvation. The jungle held all those dangers too, although there was always food and water to be found if you knew where to look; plus there were insects and animals that could poison them, creatures that could eat them, and bacteria that could just make them rot inside. And yet Peter was quietly trusting him to get them through this.

'If all else fails, we'll keep going in this direction,' Beck said, 'but if we find a stream or a river then we'll follow that. It'll head towards the sea and we can get help at a town on the coast. Rivers generally go somewhere. Follow one and you usually end up at civilization.'

'Right.' Peter still sounded quiet, subdued.

Beck shot him another look. He was hugging himself, arms wrapped around himself as if he were cold. Beck wondered if it was some kind of delayed shock, but then he noticed the anxious glances Peter was sending in every direction – up, down, all around. Now Beck thought he understood. He had felt much the same way in Borneo.

'Kind of presses in, doesn't it?' he said.

Peter immediately nodded, grateful that Beck saw it too.

It was claustrophobia. The jungle does something to your mind. You are surrounded by vegetation on all sides; you can't see the sky; in fact you can rarely see clearly for more than a couple of metres in any direction. It isn't like being in a small room, which you know you can simply step out of.

Here in this jungle, Beck knew that beyond what they could see would be miles more of the same. If you got past that bush over there, there'd just be another beyond it, and then another, and another still. That is why jungles can be such killers: they tend to just keep going on and on, with no way out. And they sap your energy so fast.

'It's all around,' Peter said. 'I mean, it's just everywhere. It's like we're at the bottom of a very deep pit . . .'

Beck realized he had to show him. 'Actually we're on quite a wide, flat bit of ground,' he said, 'but look – there's a small rise, and a much steeper bit in that direction.'

'Huh?' Peter strained his eyes into the distance but clearly couldn't see anything different.

'It's a trick you have to learn,' Beck explained. 'Don't let your eyes stop at the nearest bit of bush. Look *through* it. Don't just concentrate on what's right in front of you – that stops you seeing everything else. Look, see those ferns?'

Over to one side was what looked like a solid wall of ferns. It was a mad jumble of spiralling stalks and rough, jagged leaves.

'About halfway along, you can see they bulge out towards you.' The wall of ferns seemed to be crumbling at that point. 'They're growing up a tree and that's where the trunk is. On the right you can see it's a bit darker between the leaves than on the left. That means there's a little more open space behind it. And you can see the patterns of the leaves are going up. That means it's on sloping ground.'

'Yeah . . .' Peter said doubtfully. He looked again at the ferns. 'Maybe. If you say so.'

Beck laughed. 'You're not going to learn it immediately, but practise as we walk. We're not just surrounded by branches, right? Tell yourself that. There are thousands of different shades of light and textures and contours, and they all mean something. They tell you about where you are.'

'Still a lot of jungle,' Peter muttered defiantly, but Beck thought he heard a bit more life in his voice.

'Yeah, there is, and if we stop and mope about it, then we'll just turn into mulch like this.' He kicked at the thick carpet of leaves beneath their feet. 'So we keep moving, keep achieving something, but we also keep calm, we take our time and we keep moving at the jungle's pace, which is slow. We go round obstacles, we don't fight them. It's the *jungle*, right?' Beck smiled. 'There's plants and animals and insects and birds . . . A million different forms of life, and it's all interconnected.' Peter was chuckling at Beck's enthusiasm. 'That's why this place is so amazing—'

Just then some leaves rustled in front of them and a lizard poked its head out. One word blazed out in Beck's mind: *Food!*

CHAPTER 13

The lizard's head was about thirty centimetres long, blunt and scaly. The eyes met Beck's for just a moment and then, in a flash, the lizard turned and disappeared back into the vegetation.

Beck flung himself forward, hands outstretched. He landed on his front with an *'Oof!'* that drove the breath from his lungs, but he managed to grab hold of the tail as the rest of the lizard fought to get away into a thicket. The tail was cool and leathery in his hands. He scrambled to his knees, maintaining his grip, and dragged the lizard backwards out of the bush. Its legs scrabbled on the ground and flung a spray of torn-up leaves up into his face.

Beck stood up, a little wobbly because both

hands were occupied holding the lizard by its tail at arm's length. Immediately its feet were off the ground it stopped trying to escape. Now it just writhed, trying to arch and twist its body in order to bite him.

'Man, watch out! What is it?' Peter shouted.

'Monitor lizard.' Beck grinned and studied it as closely as he could, though he still held the wriggling creature away from him. It was an ugly animal. Its body was dark brown with white stripes and it didn't just feel like leather, it looked like it too. The scaly hide was loose and baggy, as if a small lizard had borrowed a larger lizard's skin.

'Here.' Beck angled it towards Peter. 'Take it. Hold it where I'm holding it. Mind the teeth and the claws – some of them are poisonous. Even if they aren't, there's so much bacteria in a single bite that you are going to get a serious infection.'

'OK . . .' Peter nervously reached out with both hands and took a grip just below Beck's hands. 'Weird. You sort of imagine a lizard is going to be slimy. It's dry. And cold.'

'It's cold blooded, remember?' Beck shucked his

pack off and delved into the back pocket for the glass knife. 'Keep a good hold . . .'

And with one slash he cut the lizard's throat, just behind the angle of its jaw bone. Dark blood splashed out onto the ground. The lizard twitched violently for a moment, and then went still.

'Wow.' Peter swallowed. 'Uh – a little warning next time?'

Beck grinned. 'Who to? You or the lizard?'

'Whoever . . .'

'So what exactly did you think I was going to do to it? OK, you can put it down now.'

Peter laid it on the ground and watched as Beck started cutting its head off.

'I dunno,' he said in answer to Beck's question. 'Adopt it. Teach it tricks. Call it Fido.'

'Maybe the next one. This one we're going to eat. Plenty of meat in the tail. We're lucky. I was expecting to be living off fruit and termites—'

'That's not a joke, is it?' Peter said ruefully.

Beck laughed. 'Nope. Hunting takes up a lot of energy. Fine if you were raised here in the jungle and you know all its ways. But we've got more important things to spend our energy on – like getting out. Still, if an opportunity just jumps out at you, like this guy did, you take it. There.'

He had been sawing back and forth with the knife and finally the head came free.

'Why cut off the head?'

'Like I said, a lot of bacteria on the teeth. That's where the bite is. Plus it's extra dead weight!'

Beck lowered the lizard's body into his backpack, which he zipped shut. He prodded the head with his foot. 'Give it an hour or so and the ants will have stripped that to the bone. Come on.'

As they walked on, they found the ground sloping upwards a little. It levelled out after about ten minutes into an area that was less densely planted. Peter waited while Beck scanned the ground closely, then craned his head to look up at the tree canopy.

'We've found our campsite,' he declared, sounding pleased.

'Not five o'clock yet,' Peter pointed out, checking his watch.

'Yeah, I know. But look – we're on high ground,

which means we're out of the way of flash flooding and we're less likely to be on an animal's route to water. And look up.'

Peter followed his gaze upwards but obviously couldn't see much that was important. 'More leaves,' he said, 'surprisingly like the leaves I've been seeing so much of lately.'

'Exactly. It's *just* leaves. No coconuts, no dead branches – nothing likely to fall down on us. Did you know that falling dead wood kills more people than anything else in the jungle?'

'No, I didn't know that,' Peter admitted.

'And if you look down, you'll see there are no columns of ants marching through.' Beck swung off his daysack and put it on the ground. 'I think we've earned ourselves a drink.'

Peter watched while Beck reached out for some vines that clung to the nearest tree. He checked to see he wasn't about to grab hold of a snake, then gave them a hard yank away from the trunk. Next he reached out to make a cut in one just above head height.

'Capillary action inside the vines draws the water

upwards,' he explained. 'So first you kill the action with a cut. And then . . .'

He grabbed the vine at waist level and sawed through it with the knife. Fluid started to trickle out over his hand. 'And then you let gravity do its job and the fluid flows back out.'

'Cool . . . They've all got water in them?' Peter asked, looking around at all the vines he could see. 'You mean, we're surrounded by pipes?'

'Sort of . . .' Beck cut another vine and cupped some of the fluid in his hand, sniffed, then wiped his hand dry on his trousers. 'You need to check it really is water coming out, not just sap, and if the sap is red or yellow or milky – like this – then forget it and try again.'

He had more luck with the next vine. Water dribbled out of it as if from a leaky tap. He tilted his head back and let it drip into his mouth. It was warm and musty, but it was still water.

Beck passed the vine to Peter, who almost snatched it out of his hand.

Water, Beck thought, watching his friend drink. Just a simple little chemical . . . but you couldn't even last a few days without it, and just a few drops made such a difference. He could feel the energy flowing back into him.

'Wow,' Peter gasped when the trickle from the vine finally died. 'I needed that. So what do we do next?'

'You start gathering wood for a fire. I spotted some bamboo back there – which we're going to make into a bed for the night.'

CHAPTER 14

The bamboo Beck had seen was a dense cluster wrapped in vines and clothed in spindly, dark green leaves. He cleared away the mass of foliage, once again checking for any wildlife that might lash out with a sting or a bite, to reveal the thick wooden stalks that disappeared up into the layers of canopy above. He could just get his hands around them. They were segmented, as if they had been put together from smaller wooden tubes.

Beck chose some thin young stalks and used the glass knife and the flat, sharp end of the crowbar to cut himself several pieces, each two or three metres long. Once he had sliced through them at the base, he still had to pull and shake them to free them from the grip of the vegetation higher up. Eventually he managed to drag them back to the campsite. Even though they were thin, they were strong – which is why bamboo is often used as scaffolding in the Far East.

'Beats flat-pack furniture any day,' he said cheerfully. 'It's not just pandas who find this stuff useful . . .' Beck paused. 'What's up?'

Peter was scowling. He flung a stick down on the ground so hard that it bounced. '*Gather wood for a fire*, you said. *Easy*, I thought, *we're surrounded by the stuff.*' He kicked a tree. 'But it's damp! Everything's *damp*! Look. I made a pile.' He gave the small heap of twigs a kick. 'And it's dripping. We're surrounded by wood and we can't make a fire!'

Beck carefully laid down his collection of bamboo. 'The jungle's very humid,' he said. 'You're right, it's hard to get stuff to burn here – but that's lucky, 'cos otherwise the volcano would have burned all this up long ago. But if you know where to look, you'll find that some of it's dry.'

He crouched down by a bush. Peter knelt next to him and followed his gaze. Beck reached out for the dead leaves and twigs that always hung down at the bottom.

'These will be dry.' He broke off a twig to prove it and it came away with a nice dry snap. 'Plus there'll be larger stuff, dead branches, hanging off trees. Gather those up too. And then I'll show you where to find some dry kindling.'

'OK.' Peter sounded a little more encouraged.

Beck kept one eye on him as they went to work on their separate tasks. But Peter was a quick learner and Beck was pleased to see that he had soon gathered quite a pile. He himself could get back to his own job.

First he cut one of the lengths of bamboo in half. Then he gathered up some lengths of creeper and tested it for strength, gripping it firmly in both hands and pulling. It was just as strong as a good bit of rope.

He lashed the two half-lengths of bamboo together at one end, then pulled the other ends apart to make something like a giant letter A, but without the crosspiece. Then he repeated the process, cutting another length in two and tying those pieces together as well, so that now he had two of the A-frames.

Peter had collected a decent pile of wood now and had stopped to watch him. Beck got him to hold the frames upright and propped a length of bamboo across them, connecting the tips of the two As. He used more creeper to tie them together. Now the two As could stand upright on their own, joined at the top by the crosspiece.

'We're going to need vine,' he said as he worked. 'Lots of it.'

'I'm right on it!'

Peter headed over to a thick cluster of rattan vines while Beck turned to the next stage of his work. He was still only half finished. He needed to connect the legs of the two frames with two more lengths of bamboo, each one at least thirty centimetres off the ground. These would be the bed poles.

He picked up the first length of bamboo, then stopped as he heard a scream and saw Peter leaping about halfway across the clearing. He staggered, tripped and fell over backwards.

'It moved! *It moved!*'

Beck threw down the bamboo and hurried over. 'You all right?' He held out a hand to help his friend up; he noticed he was panting and his eyes were wild.

'If it had bitten me, I'd know it, right?'

'If anything bit you, yes, you certainly would.'

Peter's panting was slowing, though he had to lean forward, resting his hands on his knees. He forced a brave smile. 'In that case it didn't bite me.' He nodded at the cluster of vines. 'Snake. In there.'

CHAPTER 15

Beck took up the crowbar and used it to poke the vines cautiously apart. If there was a poisonous snake in there, it could blunt its fangs on steel, not his hand. In amongst the vines something moved. The snake's body was a fifteen-centimetre-wide cable of solid muscle, covered in dry, waxy scales. The scales were mostly dark, with a faint diamond pattern.

Beck let his eyes follow the body – up, and then up some more. It looked like the snake was climbing the tree: its head was already much higher than the boys.

He let the vines fall back. 'It's a python,' he said, 'and quite a big one. But it's no danger to us.'

Peter bit his lip. 'From now on I'm going to take more care.'

He had stuck his hand into a clump of vines where he couldn't see what he was about to touch. In the jungle, that was always a mistake, but Beck doubted he would be doing it again in a hurry!

'Probably won't be the last of those we see, Peter,' he told his friend. 'There's well over four hundred types of snake in Indonesia. That's a lot of snakes!'

So Peter carried on cautiously, and Beck went back to the frame to finish his work.

Peter had soon cut him a good supply of rattan vine. Once you had shaved off the leaves and hooks, rattan vine was like steel cable wrapped in plastic. It almost looked man-made. Beck lashed it between the two bottom horizontal poles of the sleeping frame, over and over, until it looked like a baggy net.

'And this is our bed,' he said proudly. He stepped back to admire his handiwork. It was a sleeping platform held off the ground, away from ants and scorpions, by the two A-frames at either end. Even snakes would be more likely to crawl under it than go up.

Peter looked at it without much enthusiasm.

'Those creepers are going to dig in,' he pointed out.

'It's under control,' Beck assured him. 'Still a couple of things to do . . . Why don't you start the fire?'

'Where's the nice dry kindling you mentioned?'

'Right here.' Beck knelt down by some of the bamboo he wasn't using and scraped the glass knife across it. The outer layer was waxy and glistened with moisture, but as damp peelings curled away beneath the blade, they exposed wood beneath that was yellow and bone-dry.

Beck handed the knife to his friend. 'Shave off some of that, and you've got your kindling.'

'Cool!' Peter went to work.

Beck could very easily have made the fire on his own, and in half the time, but he wanted to keep Peter busy; his help was valuable and Beck wanted him to know it.

Peter had picked up a lot of cool survival tips from Beck over the years. Now he showed he had remembered some of them himself. He used the knife to cut some of the seat stuffing up into shreds and gathered it up into a small pile a few centimetres high. He laid the shaved bamboo kindling on top of this. Finally, above that, he made a small pyramid of dry sticks and twigs that he had collected with Beck's guidance. There was still a larger pile of sticks left over to feed the fire with.

Meanwhile Beck had cut down a clump of palm leaves. Some of these he laid across the vine hammock he had made. Peter had been right – they would dig in, but the palm leaves would act as a very basic mattress.

Beck had other uses planned for the leaves. They were long and thin, and seen in cross-section, they were v-shaped. He laid these along the horizontal top pole of the sleeping frame, from one end to the other, to act as a makeshift roof. But the roof had another purpose as well. Beck took one last length of bamboo and used the crowbar to split it from end to end, into two halves. He was left with two rough half-tubes of wood, each divided into sections. The cut wasn't very smooth, but the halves would hold water, which was the main thing.

'Guttering?' Peter asked. He had finished his task

first and was watching Beck, lending a hand when needed.

'Yup.' Beck laid the half-tubes on the ground alongside the frame, and positioned them under the ends of the overhanging palm leaves. 'When it rains – and it will rain, 'cos this is a rainforest – the leaves will keep the water off us, but it'll also flow down them into these. And in the morning we fill our bottles and drink it. How's the fire?'

Peter stood proudly by the pile. 'All ready for you to light.'

'Well, OK, but . . .' Beck felt for the cord round his neck. 'Why don't you do the honours?'

Peter's eyes lit up. 'Really?'

'You've watched me do it enough times.' Beck pulled his fire steel over his head and chucked it over.

CHAPTER 16

The fire steel, Beck's most vital possession, consisted of a small metal rod and a flat steel square. The rod was made of ferrosium, a volatile combination of metals that gave off extremely hot sparks whenever it was scraped with something hard and sharp. That was what the steel square was for. Beck had taken it with him all over the world.

The principle was simple, but the technique needed some practice. With each scrape the ferrosium sheered off sparks, and in the gloom beneath the trees it gave off an orange light that was quite spectacular. But they didn't have time to admire it: both boys were huddled over the small pile of tinder and kindling, willing the sparks to catch.

Just as Peter was beginning to get frustrated, a flurry of orange sparks showered down, and a small corner of the stuffing started to smoulder. Immediately Peter leaned close and blew on it gently, giving it a steady supply of oxygen to turn the embers into a flame. Finally the stuffing caught light. It slowly grew into a glowing ball of fibres, and then the bamboo began to catch too. The shavings curled slowly in the heat, blackening in the flame. And finally the flame reached the sticks.

Beck always reckoned a fire was a success when he heard that *crack* – the distinct sound wood makes when water trapped inside it turns to steam and bursts out under the pressure. More and more cracks sounded as the flames spread up through the pile. The warmth beat against the boys' faces. An equatorial rainforest is not a cold place, but this warmth was comforting. It was dry and hot and life-giving. Just the sight of a good fire, Beck had always found, raised his spirits.

'Supper time!' he announced. He unzipped his daysack and pulled out the dead lizard. The smell of blood and dead meat came out with it.

'Man alive.' Peter pulled a face. 'I think your pack's going to need a wash, Beck.'

'Maybe I'll just give this one to you as a present – if we get out of this mess, that is!' Beck held the lizard up for inspection. It hadn't had time to go off in the time since he killed it, and because he had kept his pack zipped up, the flies hadn't been able to get at it. 'Could you set up a spit?' he asked. 'A couple of tall sticks either side of the fire and a horizontal piece over the top . . .'

While Peter did that, Beck cut the lizard open with the knife, being careful not to puncture any internal organs. If he cut into the stomach or the intestines, the acid would leak out and ruin the good meat. It wasn't hard to avoid them, though. The lizard's body wasn't tightly packed, like a mammal's. It felt like a leather bag of innards, and you could tell what was where just by feel.

Beck was only after one thing here, and that was the liver, three quarters of the way down the body. It was the size of his fist, clammy and dark rusty brown. When he pulled it out of the lizard's abdomen, it glistened in the firelight. The bile sac clung to it and looked like an abnormal green growth. Bile was disgustingly bitter, not something Beck wanted to eat. The rest of the liver, though, would be rich in iron and nutrients, and pretty tasty once cooked. Beck carefully cut the bile sac away and set the liver aside. He threw the sac into the undergrowth.

Finally he sliced off the lizard's tail. There would be nothing else in the body worth eating, but the tail was almost solid meat. The skin was tough and almost fireproof, so he left it on. They could cook the meat in the skin and remove the outer layer when it was done. He threw the body well away from the camp. It would attract armies of ants, and he didn't want to lead them to where he and Peter would be sleeping.

Meanwhile Peter had set up the spit. Beck skewered the tail and the liver on a long stick and propped it up over the flames. The two friends then used more sticks to sweep the ground clear of leaves and anything else that might be lurking; finally they sat on either side of the fire and watched the meat cook.

'End of the first day,' Beck said cheerfully. 'Nothing's eaten us yet.'

'Uh-huh.' Peter sat and hugged his knees, and looked thoughtfully into the flames.

Beck sensed his friend wasn't quite as cheerful as he was. 'We're going to be all right, buddy – you know that?'

Peter looked up, his expression serious. 'Yeah. I know.'

'What are you thinking?' Beck asked gently.

Peter sighed. 'Just remembering Nakula. And wondering about Mum and Dad. We were meant to be getting back to Medan about now, so they'll soon work out we're late. And if they haven't already heard about the volcano, they soon will. And then they'll be going out of their minds with worry. OK, they know about you – they know you can survive just about anywhere, and if I'm with you they'll know I'll probably be OK . . . but what about Nakula's family? If he had one. They said goodbye to him this morning like normal and now they're . . . they're never going to see him again . . . It's too awful . . .'

Beck thought of his own parents. He had waved them off at the start of a perfectly normal trip – and never seen them again either. 'Awful' didn't even begin to describe it.

'I see my mum and dad every day,' Beck whispered gently. Peter looked up at him in surprise. 'Every time I do something they taught me or I see some difference they made in my life. I always feel Mum around me. I bet you, in time, Nakula's family will find that too. I mean, hearing someone you love has died is the worst thing ever, and that never goes away, but think of the difference he made. Think of the sanctuary.'

'I'm so sorry about your mum and dad, Beck. I never really said that properly before.'

Beck smiled at Peter warmly. Until someone close to you actually died it was impossible to know what it was like. Beck prayed his friend wouldn't have to find out for many years.

'Hey, Peter, your parents are going to be so proud of us,' he told him, lightening the tone. 'They'll realize we had no option but to head into the jungle. And we are going to get through this. Sure, it's not going to be like a walk in the park back home, but if we stick together and work together, we'll survive. Just like in the Sahara. What's important is that we focus on getting through this *alive*.'

Peter's smile in the firelight was warm and genuine. 'Yeah, we'll do that,' he said confidently.

Beck felt his own heart lift as well. 'But we should get some sleep,' he added.

Climbing onto the sleeping frame took some careful manoeuvring. It creaked and groaned with their weight, but it held together. The boys lay head to toe and back to back on a thin mattress of palm leaves.

'Beck?' Peter murmured after a few minutes.

'Uh-huh?'

'What about tigers? This thing isn't exactly a cage, is it?'

Beck had mentioned earlier that they were in tiger territory. They hadn't discussed this since. There hadn't seemed much point. It wouldn't change anything.

'Tigers are very solitary,' Beck told his friend. 'The chances of one wandering past us in the night are pretty slim.'

107

'Oh.' Peter was quiet for a moment or two. 'And anyway, I guess they'll be asleep soon, like us?'

'They're nocturnal—' Beck started to correct him, but stopped when he realized what he was saying.

Peter sighed. 'You know, that's really not comforting!'

CHAPTER 17

Despite his worries (and the fact that the creepers *did* dig in, leaves or no leaves), Peter had dropped off almost immediately. He was worn out in body and mind, and he had a good meal of lizard inside him to digest. Beck lay awake for a little while longer, listening to the jungle. It was like a living creature all around them. Crackles and crunches, whoops and whistles – a million life forms getting on with the business of living and dying. But at some point sleep took him too.

It was a rumble of thunder that woke him up, briefly. The fire had gone out and it was pitch dark. Rain drummed down relentlessly all around them. It pattered on the roof of palm leaves above, and he could hear streams of water pouring into his bamboo water collectors. Drops of it inevitably got through and landed on him, but he could live with that. Beyond the roof of the A-frame he could hear it hammering down. It washed the air clean, and made it fresh and cool once more. It was like being surrounded by an invisible waterfall.

The sound of the rain finally sent him back to sleep again.

They woke up early the next day, their second day in the jungle. The moment he was awake, Beck felt an extra layer of slick sweat clinging to his body. The freshness of the night's rain was already a memory. The sun had come up as quickly as it went down, and the moisture left by the rain was now turning to steam.

Beck swung his legs down and reached for his shoes beneath the sleeping frame. They had left their shoes propped upside down on sticks, to keep them dry. He gave each one a shake and looked carefully inside before putting it on. When he shook the second one, a scorpion as long as his middle finger fell out. Beck watched it scuttle away as he laced up his shoes. He smiled, grateful for the advice his father had given him about always checking inside your shoes first thing in the morning.

He bent over to touch his toes, then stood up straight and rotated his arms like a windmill for a few seconds. A stab of pain reminded him of his cut: he needed to change the bandage. Meanwhile he felt the blood and energy start to flow back into his sleepy muscles.

Beck was pleased to see the water collectors were brimming with clear, fresh water.

Peter twitched and stirred. 'Ugh.' His mouth was dry and sticky; he had to swallow a couple of times just to be able to speak. 'Aching. And thirsty.'

'Better get up, then. There's plenty of water.'

While Peter got up, Beck filled the bottles from the collectors. As he carefully poured out the half-bamboos' contents, he savoured the *glug-glug* sound.

Beck passed a bottle to Peter, who drank almost half of it in a couple of swallows.

'I could just keep drinking and never stop.'

'You're not wrong,' Beck replied. 'We need to drink whenever we can. The humidity means we're going to sweat a lot. It's like a steam bath already and it's only going to get worse. You only need two and a half per cent less water in your body to make it twenty-five per cent less efficient, and we're going to need all our strength today.'

'So . . .' Peter quickly did the sums in his head. 'Ten per cent less water and you just grind to a halt.'

'I think you'd be dead before then.'

'Yeah, but think of the advantages. If you had ten per cent less water – or even less than that – you could be sort of freeze-dried. Then someone else carries you through the jungle and they just add water at the end of the trip to restore you.'

'Keep having good ideas like that,' Beck promised with a straight face, 'and you'll be a millionaire before you're twenty.'

'I'll cut you in on the deal,' Peter assured him. 'I'm also going to launch a new range of jungle survival food. Lizard tails, still in their own skin, available at your local supermarket. I'll grow them in vats.'

'Yeah?' Beck rummaged in his pack for the crowbar. 'Don't forget the new, healthy jungle breakfast range. More protein per ounce than beef.'

Beck's smile widened as his friend's froze. Reality crowded in on Peter's fantasy.

'And that would be . . . ?' he asked reluctantly.

Beck led the way over to a fallen log near their camp. The outer layers of bark were rotten and loose. He dug the crowbar in and levered them off. A few dozen insects and grubs scuttled and writhed around in protest.

'Insects. Of course.'

'You've eaten them before,' Beck pointed out. In the Sahara they had eaten spiders, grubs, scorpions . . .

'Well, yeah, I've also fallen off my bike and broken my arm before. Doesn't mean I want to make a habit of it,' Peter replied, quick as a flash.

He came over and looked down at the breakfast spread without enthusiasm. Then he sighed and picked up a large grub between thumb and forefinger. 'What's this one?'

Beck studied it. It was as thick as a finger, a translucent blue-white, and curled like a prawn. 'Beetle larva, I think. Don't eat the head. Hold it there and bite the rest of it off.'

'OK, here goes . . .' Peter screwed his eyes shut and bit into the larva. He chewed it and swallowed, eyes still closed.

Beck remembered the very first time he had tried eating grubs. It had been in Australia – how could he ever forget the feeling in his mouth – the slight resistance of the flesh before it burst between his teeth, the explosion of goo, like rotting fish. And of course, Beck's father had been there, reminding him just as he was about to remind Peter.

'Good on you, buddy. We need all the nourishment we can get,' he said. 'And we definitely can't afford to be squeamish in a survival situation.'

'Yeah, I know . . .' Peter opened his eyes thoughtfully. 'Y'know . . . it's not actually that bad.' He scooped up three or four more in his cupped hand and ate them one at a time.

'Hey, don't take the lot!'

When they had eaten as many as they could find, Beck poured water on his bandaged arm, gently moistening the wound. Then he slowly peeled off the bandage, wincing as it ripped at the congealed blood. The cut was still open, glistening, and the flesh on either side of it was red and tender.

'I think a doctor would want to put a stitch in that,' said Peter, peering at it.

'That's beyond our resources,' Beck muttered. 'Though I've heard of jungle tribes using soldier ants . . .'

'Huh?' Peter was cutting another strip off the spare T-shirt for a bandage. 'How?'

'Soldier ants have jaws a centimetre wide. You hold them over the cut so that when they bite you, they actually pull the edges of the cut together. Then you twist their bodies off and the heads stay in.'

'*Ow!*'

'Exactly. But we might not have any choice if this gets any worse . . .'

Peter wrapped the new bandage round the cut and Beck pulled his sleeve down over it.

'And I suppose,' Peter pointed out as they set off into the jungle again, 'you could always eat the ant bodies . . .'

'We're gonna make a jungle guide of you soon at this rate, Peter!'

CHAPTER 18

Beck's plan was to eat and drink as they went. If they stopped at all, it would only be briefly. Eating on the move meant they covered more ground, and it suited the 'little and often' philosophy. They would take in enough energy to keep them going but not so much that their bodies would start to divert the precious water and energy needed to digest a large meal. And eating on the move gave them something to focus on beyond their immediate predicament.

Sometimes food just presented itself, like a cluster of low-hanging figs. Fig trees in the jungle are distinctive: straggly, with aerial roots – knobbly pro-trusions just like the roots you find below ground, but taking moisture in from the damp air. The leaves are leathery and evergreen, with rounded bases. The figs look like green balls growing straight out of the plant and can be eaten raw.

There was plenty of fallen, rotting wood around, and that meant plenty more insects. Peter seemed to be getting quite into insects, which surprised Beck. He secretly hated them, eating them purely out of necessity.

Beck couldn't help noticing that his friend seemed to have more of a spring in his step today. He was looking around, taking an interest in his surroundings, even if his glasses were fogged up with steam most of the time. Everything that had happened yesterday – the volcano, the crash, Nakula being killed – had been a shock. In their hurry to get away from the volcano and set up a camp for the night they'd had very little time to come to terms with their situation.

Beck remembered Peter's attack of claustrophobia. Yesterday, the jungle had been an oppressive, threatening place. Today it still wasn't exactly *safe* – if they ever made the mistake of thinking that, it could be fatal – but Peter seemed to have accepted it.

A crumbling, thirty-metre-long tree trunk lay across their path. It was another type of palm, with long thin leaves neatly spaced along its branches.

'Hey, more food?' Peter asked hopefully.

Beck laughed. 'Could be . . . In fact, definitely. I think this is a sago palm. And that means palm grubs.'

He used the crowbar to lever away the rotten bark, as before, then hacked into the wood. He prised out a chunk of the tree's heartwood and spotted something trying to wriggle out of sight. Beck dug it out and held it up. It looked like a giant maggot, three or four centimetres long.

'Definitely palm grubs,' he confirmed. 'You can eat 'em raw or cooked, depending. We'll gather some up for later when we've got a fire.'

And so they dug out a handful more, putting them into one of the pockets of Peter's pack for safe-keeping. Then something else caught Beck's eye.

He strolled over to what seemed to be a giant brown growth on the side of a tree. It obviously wasn't part of the tree itself. It looked like an enormous mole or scab.

'Termite nest,' he called over his shoulder to Peter, who was still gathering insects. Beck dug the knife into the brown mass, and a clump of wriggling, translucent creatures fell out onto his hand and arm. He quickly brushed them away.

'Don't let them get onto you or they'll infest you – hair, privates, everything. But they're good eating.' He popped a couple straight into his mouth and chewed. There was definite *zing* to termites – a bit like slightly off citrus fruit; something in the region of old orange or lemon. But it was still nicer than the grubs they had eaten earlier. 'One good thing about them – you'll never run short. There's thousands in this one nest. They're a vital part of the jungle – they digest all that rotting wood, and then recycle it!'

'There's some interesting-looking ones here too,' Peter added.

Beck popped another couple of termites into his mouth; there was no point wasting the opportunity. Then, from behind him, he heard:

'Mm, smells like marzipan!'

An alarm bell rang in Beck's head. Before he even knew it, he was running back to Peter – who was holding up a very long, black and red millipede, as thick as a finger and as long as a hand. Its thousands of segments made it look like an evil armour-plated CGI war robot from a trashy science fiction movie. It writhed and twisted in Peter's grip, and what looked like thousands of little legs waved impotently. It might have been the legs that had stopped Peter trying to swallow it. He was about to bite it in half instead.

'Stop!' Beck swatted his friend's hand and the millipede flew away.

Peter stared at him as if he had gone mad. 'What?'

'Did any of it get into your mouth? Anything at all?'

'No, nothing. Why?'

The millipede hadn't got far. It was heading slowly and steadily back into the undergrowth. Beck picked it up again and sniffed it. Peter was right – there was a distinct smell of marzipan.

'That's not marzipan . . .' Beck's voice was a little shaky. He didn't like near misses. 'This kind of bug secretes cyanide as a defence mechanism. Cyanide smells like almonds. Like marzipan.'

The symptoms of cyanide poisoning. His medical instructor marched through his memories again. *Seizures. Cardiac arrest. Coma. Death . . .*

Beck added quietly, 'Definitely not edible!'

Peter was pale. 'Wow. I almost ate it . . .'

Beck remembered his friend's new-found confidence. He didn't want Peter losing that again. 'Yeah, well, you're still alive!' He chucked the millipede as far away as he could and wiped his hand on his trousers. 'Hey, fancy some citrus . . . ?'

A couple of minutes later Peter admitted, between mouthfuls, that he much preferred lemony termites to cyanide-emitting armour-plated millipedes.

'And there's another thing . . .' Beck passed his pack to Peter. 'Hold this open for me, under the nest . . .'

Peter did so, and Beck cut away a section of nest so that it fell straight into the pack.

'The nest burns nicely and the smoke keeps mosquitoes away,' he explained. 'We can use this wherever we end up this evening.'

'I think I read somewhere that termites make their nests out of their own excretions?'

'Yup,' Beck said with a grin as he zipped up his pack. 'I believe they do.'

'So, burning termite poo?'

'The new scent for men! C'mon, let's keep going.'

CHAPTER 19

Beck maintained a constant, steady pace to press on through the jungle. It meant they covered ground but they didn't get the break or respite that both of them soon craved. Meanwhile Beck's arm was throbbing. Clammy sweat soaked every inch of him and he could feel the salt stinging the gash. Struggling through the jungle made his back and legs ache – the constant bending down, straightening up and twisting round; you could never just *walk*.

He thought of all the jungle movies he had seen where the heroes boldly slashed their way through the undergrowth. In fact, as Beck well knew, the real way to negotiate the dense jungle is not to fight your way through it, but to become cat-like, stealthy, easing your way through the vegetation. But sometimes the whole jungle just grows together into one big tangled knot and you grind to a halt.

'Can I hear water?' Peter asked suddenly.

Beck stopped and cocked his head. Peter had been following on behind without complaint. He hadn't noticed anything in particular about the jungle, apart from the fact that it was getting thicker and harder work. But he was certain he had heard the sound of running water.

Both boys stood motionless in the tangled jungle, listening.

All at once Beck felt a huge wave of relief wash over him. Peter was right. Through the bushes he could hear a distinct trickling, splashing noise like one pipe pouring into another.

'Well done, Peter. Quick. Follow me. It's this way.'

It only took another minute of thrashing and twisting through the undergrowth, and then the boys were standing at the edge of a small river.

The splashing sound came from the far bank, where another stream dropped down from some slightly higher ground in a metre-high waterfall. The water bubbled and chuckled where the two flows met.

'Whoa!' Peter exclaimed. He craned his head back. 'I can see the sky!'

The sky was a blue strip through the jungle canopy. The vegetation came down almost to the water's edge. There was a narrow strip of river bank, sand and gravel, and then the river was a five-metre-wide watery highway. It flowed from right to left, the waters slow and brown. With no trees to block it there was also a slight breeze – it was still hot and humid, but the air felt a little fresher simply because it was moving.

Beck looked on the river like a gift from above. Gratitude swelled in his heart. This was good in so many ways.

'We can make our way along the bank,' he said, 'or even in the shallows. Easier than fighting our way through the jungle! And the great thing about rivers is that they often lead to people. If we follow it, we'll either reach the sea or a town . . .' His voice trailed off thoughtfully and he started to look up and down the river very, very carefully.

'All the water we can drink,' Peter pointed out, though his voice was distracted. He held his arms up in front of his face and studied them closely. Beck could see the mottled red skin. 'I think I'm getting a heat rash.'

'It's sweat build-up. All that salt and gunge going nowhere.' Beck took one more look at the river, first downstream, then up. He couldn't see any signs of what he was searching for, so he relaxed and started to unbutton his shirt. 'We should take every chance we can to wash – let's do it!'

His first thought was to check on his wounded arm again. The bandage had to be soaked off and the cut looked just as open and raw as before. With all that salty sweat getting into it, Beck wasn't surprised it wasn't healing. He cupped water in his left hand and poured it up and down the cut to wash the grime out.

Then he scooped up handfuls of grit and rubbed them up and down his arms and legs. He could feel the rough mixture scraping off the grime that seemed to cake him; it left his skin feeling fresh and tingling. 'Try it!' he told Peter. 'It's nature's exfoliator!' Again, though, he checked up and down the river.

This time Peter was watching him. 'What are you looking for?'

'Crocodiles.'

Peter stopped rubbing and took several steps back from the river.

Beck kept talking as he rubbed himself down. 'They love rivers like this. Murky water, slow flow, and packed with fish no doubt. They're responsible for so many attacks on unsuspecting humans, you can't be too careful.'

Peter winced, before saying, 'I saw one in a zoo in Sydney once – and I was so glad there were several centimetres of armoured glass between us. It was just lying there – until feeding time, when they dropped a lump of meat in and it lunged faster than you could see. The keepers told us they can swim at something like twenty miles an hour, and when they bite, those jaws pack about three thousand pounds per square inch.'

'And once they've got you,' Beck added, 'you aren't going to escape. They death roll you, drag you underwater and leave you under some log until you rot and they can eat you . . .'

Peter's mouth was hanging open and he looked a little green. Beck realized that his information wasn't helping Peter's confidence any.

He smiled and went on, 'So, anyway, look out for them. They lie underwater with just their eyes sticking out . . .'

After that, Peter kept his gaze fixed firmly on the water.

* * *

The rub-down left them both feeling cleaner and refreshed. They soaked their clothes and wrung them out as hard as they could. They were still damp when they put them back on, but at least fresh water had now replaced the sweat.

Then they set off along the river, heading downstream. The brief break had lifted their spirits considerably. Sometimes the river dropped down a couple of metres, coursing over smooth rocks that the boys had to clamber down. Sometimes the banks narrowed, forcing them to wade through the water instead, sending sheets of spray up into the air.

Even when it came up to their knees, it was much easier than clambering through the jungle.

'And another thing,' Peter added, as if he had been giving the matter deep thought. 'If the tigers are anything like our cat at home, they won't be following us here! He hates water.'

Beck grimaced. 'Yeah, but Sumatran tigers have one thing Tiddles doesn't . . .'

'What's that?' Peter asked suspiciously.

'Webbed feet.'

'You're kidding!'

'Nope. They evolved in swampy ground. They don't mind the water at all.'

'Oh, great . . .' Peter scanned the jungle on either side, as if expecting half a ton of striped muscle to leap out at them at any moment.

'Hey, don't sweat it. The tigers'll be asleep at this time of day. What we really want to look out for now is crocodiles, especially as it looks like the river is widening.'

'Lurking just beneath the surface . . .' Peter said.

'With their eyes sticking out,' Beck agreed.

Peter came to a complete halt, and nodded over

at the far side of the river. 'Like that?' he asked quietly.

It looked like a log drifting towards them, a small lump of wood jutting above the surface. But it wasn't a lump of wood: it had two cold, unblinking reptilian eyes. And behind it, only the slightest ripple gave away the five metres of crocodile that was cruising slowly down the river towards them.

CHAPTER 20

'Yes,' Beck murmured. 'Like that.'

The boys stood very still. They were up to their knees in the shallows.

The crocodile's dark hide made it almost exactly the same colour as the river. You could imagine it was just a lump of slightly more solid water that was cruising gently by. The line of ripples were the ridges along the croc's back. Its tail moved silently from side to side as it propelled itself downstream. It was incredible that anything as hard and knobbly could move through the water so effortlessly.

And Beck had just a few seconds to decide what to do. His thoughts raced through the options. Run? Stay? Climb a tree? Crocodiles like to sneak up on you and pounce from a very short range. This one was still only halfway across the river.

OK. He tried to say it, but his mouth was too dry. He had to swallow to get some spit going so his words would come out. He tried again.

'OK. I'll count to three and then we run. You go left, I'll go right . . .'

'We can't outrun it.' Peter was as white as a sheet; his eyes were fixed on the approaching reptile. 'You said.'

Beck remembered Peter happily telling him that these things could swim at twenty miles per hour. That meant it could cover the distance between them in a few seconds.

'You don't need to outrun it,' he pointed out. 'You just need to outrun me.'

Peter looked at him, aghast, then quickly turned back to the crocodile.

Beck repeated: 'Ready to run? It can only chase one of us.'

'Oh dear God . . .' Peter mumbled.

Beck stared into the croc's eyes. He could imagine little red laser dots on his and Peter's chests.

The crocodile's food detection system had locked on. It wanted one of these skinny hairless apes in its larder at the bottom of the river. It would wedge their bodies under a rock or a sunken log. They would rot away in the water. Their flesh would drift loose from the bones until eventually it was tender and tasty enough to be devoured.

'One . . .' he said. Peter tensed. 'Two . . .'

A whoop and the gibbering of many voices made Beck look away from the croc and across the river. A group of dark furred apes had swung down from the trees to the water's edge. They were on the far side of the river, a bit further down. They looked like a cross between an orang-utan, with its long arms, and a chimpanzee. Beck recognized them as siamangs, a kind of gibbon.

There were five or six of them. Beck remembered that they travelled in families. There would be a dominant adult male and female, and their offspring, and maybe a couple of teenagers waiting to be dominant adults themselves. It wasn't hard to spot the two adults. They were larger and they waited at the back, one perched on a log, the other up in a tree. They kept a suspicious eye out for danger while the rest crouched by the edge of the river and drank.

But the lookouts weren't doing a very good job because the crocodile had changed course. It was heading straight for them. There was barely a ripple now – even the eyes had submerged.

The boys stared, transfixed.

It was like being a witness to a murder. Beck's heart pounded, knowing what would come. He wanted to shout a warning, throw a stone, do something to warn the helpless prey. But he was only too well aware that the croc might just go back to plan A, eating the hairless ape that had spoiled its meal.

Then, in the blink of an eye, the crocodile lurched forward in an explosion of spray. A huge sheet of water splashed up into the air and hid the details. There was a glimpse of the croc's body, long, armoured and deadly; a dim impression of panicking, scattered furry bodies. By the time the spray dropped back into the river it was over. There was just a final impression of jaws clamped over a siamang, and the gibbon screaming before the water closed over its head.

The other siamangs shrieked and howled their protest. They stood on the river bank and leaped up and down, baring their teeth and thumping their chests and the ground. They looked and sounded fearsome, and the display would have scared off just about anyone . . . except for a crocodile that really didn't care what the gibbons thought. It had already got what it wanted.

'Let's get out of the water,' Beck said quietly. Peter just nodded and turned towards the bank.

Beck bit his lip. That had been way, way too close. He should have known better. He knew what killing machines crocodiles were. Kill, eat and make baby crocodiles – that was a croc's entire life. He knew how well they could hide in a muddy river. If those gibbons hadn't been there to distract the croc . . .

It was one more example of what he was always telling himself anyway. You had to *take care*. Be constantly on the lookout. Keep thinking. Keep alert. Never let your guard down.

They clambered back up the bank.

'OK, we'll still follow the river . . . but from now on we won't get too close, right?'

Beck felt the water slosh about in his waterlogged shoes. It gushed and gurgled around his toes like an extra layer of slime.

Peter had the same problem. His feet made the kind of noise you usually only hear from the rear end of a well-fed cow. 'Squelch, squelch, squelch . . .' he said, and it seemed much funnier than it should. It punctured the tension of their narrow escape from the croc. Deep down, both boys knew they had got lucky.

'We need to get our shoes off for a moment.' Beck checked a log and sat down on it to untie his laces. Then he held each shoe upside down so that the water could drain out. But instead of putting them back on, he got the glass knife and used it to poke holes in the side of each one, just above the instep. The leather put up a brief resistance but then the point of the glass slid in smoothly. He saw Peter's enquiring glance.

'We need shoes to protect our feet,' he explained, 'but if we walk around with water in them we'll end up with trench foot. Ever had athlete's foot?'

'Yeah, a couple of times.'

'It's about ten times worse. You get blisters and sores, which turn into fungal infections, which turn into gangrene. Give it a few days and your feet could need amputating.'

'And I suppose you'd eat them too,' Peter said thoughtfully.

Beck pulled a face. 'You're sick!'

Peter laughed.

'Just give me your shoes . . .'

CHAPTER 21

Beck glanced at his watch. It was mid-afternoon, about twenty-four hours after the crash that had got them into this situation. That was food for thought. Twenty-four hours and they still hadn't seen anyone else. They had to see signs of people eventually. But right now all Beck could see was jungle and more jungle.

Give it another hour, he decided, and they would call a halt for the day.

'Listen!' Peter stopped dead in his tracks. A faint rumble drifted down through the canopy. He looked at Beck with wide eyes. 'That wasn't another eruption, was it?'

'No,' Beck replied, looking aloft. 'That was—'

Suddenly it started to rain.

Rain in a rainforest was like someone in the sky turning on a tap. Back home there would be a few tentative drops. They would gradually get stronger until someone noticed. Here it was either raining or it wasn't. There was no in-between. And when it did rain, it was like every drop of moisture in existence was just dumping itself out of the sky on top of you.

'. . . rain,' Beck finished.

Even with the shelter of the tree canopy, it was only about ten seconds before the boys were completely soaked. Beck felt his hair plastered against his head. His clothes were as wet and clinging as if he had just jumped into a river. Peter's glasses had turned into steamy circles.

The jungle was already dim. The rain made it even gloomier. They needed shelter and there was no point in waiting any longer. Beck decided to use the available light now – before it got too dark.

'We need somewhere to make camp.'

'You going to make another sleeping frame?'

'I suppose. We'll need more bamboo . . .'

Beck looked around. A bamboo cluster a short distance away was a likely looking candidate, but his attention was caught by what was next to it. It was a tall tree – he wasn't quite sure what type – with a trunk so thick he couldn't have put his arms around it. And about halfway up, in the fork of some branches, was what looked like a pile of driftwood.

'Hey.' He nudged Peter. 'Does that look familiar?'

But Peter was blind with his glasses on in the rain, and was busily trying to wipe them.

'Wait here . . .' Beck told him.

The tree trunk was encrusted with old vines, thick and secure enough to provide footholds. Beck clambered up quickly while rain sluiced down all around him, taking care to keep three points fixed at all times. It only took him thirty seconds to reach the fork in the branches.

Where they met they formed a shallow bowl in the trunk. It was not quite flat but it was wide enough for two people. And someone – or more accurately some*thing* – had laid down a pile of logs and leaves to pad the bowl out a bit and create more room.

'It's an orang-utan nest!' he called down to Peter excitedly. Rain thudded onto the branches and the leaves around him and he had to raise his voice. 'Ready made!'

He was amused to see that the branches of a fig tree were intertwined with this one, and there were clusters of figs within easy reach. He remembered what Nakula had said about the lazy orang-utans.

The nest hadn't been used recently. The wood was old, the leaves withered. The boys could use it without being thrown out by an irate owner who was twice as strong as them. And the position was good. Not so high up as to be really dangerous but well off the ground and out of harm's way.

Beck started to climb back down again.

'Not very sheltered, is it?' Peter pointed out when Beck reached the ground. He had put his glasses away and was peering up at the nest short-sightedly. Rain spattered against his upturned face.

'Not yet,' Beck corrected him. 'That'll change. Look, could you start searching for more firewood? Like last night?'

Peter raised an eyebrow and looked around the sopping wet jungle.

'Look in the same places,' Beck told him

patiently. 'Under bushes, under leaves – some of it will still be dry. Put it straight in your pack to keep it that way. And I'll see about the shelter.'

The nest was going to need a roof, and the narrow palm leaves Beck had used the previous night probably wouldn't do the trick. While Peter looked for dry wood, Beck scouted about until he found some wild bananas. The banana bush was matted and intertwined with half a dozen other types of plant, but the leaves made it stand out. They were almost as long as he was, and nearly as wide. He cut off a cluster of them and brought them back to the foot of the big tree. Then he went back to pick a couple of bunches of wild bananas. They were smaller than the bananas back home but grew in much bigger clumps, twenty or thirty at a time.

'Plenty of energy,' he explained to Peter. 'And we've got plenty of water to wash them down with!'

Peter eloquently looked up at the rain that was still falling out of the sky. 'But we've got to catch it somehow.'

'I've got an even better way.'

Beck turned his attention to the bamboo cluster

he had seen earlier. The segmented stalks were old and large. The waxy wood had mellowed from green to yellow. He tapped one of the sections experimentally, and it made a resonant *bonk*. He tapped another, nearer the top. This one had broken off higher up and he could see the jagged end above his head. Its noise was slightly different. *Bunk!*

'You going to play a tune?'

'They sound different because one of them is full of water,' Beck explained.

CHAPTER 22

Beck kept tapping the bamboos and several of the lower segments sounded full. It wasn't possible to cut them very neatly – he didn't have the tools to saw along the join where the segments met. Instead, he had to hack away with the crowbar, but by the end of it he had two rough, jagged, but intact segments. They were each about half a metre long. When he proudly held them up to Peter and shook them, they could hear the water slosh about inside.

'We won't get thirsty!' he said.

Beck also set up another water collector, but unlike the previous night, he just stamped his shoe into the ground to make a hole about the size of a football, and then moulded several banana leaves across it. The hole began to fill up even before he'd finished.

Finally it was time to haul everything up to the nest. Beck pulled down more lengths of rattan vine, the cable of the jungle. These he coiled and carefully hung across Peter's shoulders. Then he stood and watched as Peter started to climb, and gave advice about where to find foot- and handholds. Peter was a slow and nervous climber but the tree was relatively easy to scale.

'OK! Good job,' Beck called once Peter was safely perched in the nest. 'Now throw the vine down.'

There was a pause, and then the entire coil landed at his feet. Beck put his hands on his hips and glared up. Peter's apologetic face appeared over the edge of the nest.

'Oh. You meant hang onto one end of it, didn't you?'

And so Beck climbed the tree again, taking the vine back up, while raindrops as big as bumblebees splashed down around him. Then he climbed back to the ground, tied the banana leaves and the bamboo sections together, and Peter hauled them up to the nest while Beck climbed up for a third time.

It was still raining, but not as heavily. Even so, Beck's first job was to get some kind of roof up. Just because the rain had stopped now didn't mean it wouldn't rain again. This was the jungle, after all.

A branch stuck out above the nest, about a metre and a half above their heads. Beck used this as a support for the roof. He could split the stems of the banana leaves and then drape them over the branch. It meant they had a sloping roof and the rain would drip down on either side of them. They were still wet, but at least they wouldn't be getting any *wetter*.

'And the final touch, at least until the engineer comes round to install our broadband connection – the fire!' Beck said.

Peter sat with his knees hugged to his chest and watched Beck prepare the small pile. Seat stuffing, like the previous night, and bamboo shavings. The fire steel sparked and cast an orange light over Beck's face every time he struck it. And struck it again. This fire was very reluctant to catch.

'I can't believe we're lighting a *fire* in a *tree*,' Peter commented.

'*Trying* to light,' Beck corrected him under his breath.

He grimaced with frustration. The kindling was dry but the air feeding it was not. He would strike sparks and they would take root in the stuffing and glow for a few moments. Then they would die away again.

Eventually he simply went into overdrive, striking the fire steel over and over and over again until a whole cloud of sparks fell down onto the pile. Lots of sparks worked where one spark had failed. The pile couldn't help taking the hint that it was meant to burn. First a red glow crept along a strand of stuffing. Then it passed onto another strand, and then another.

'Thank God for that,' Beck sighed. 'Now let's build it up and then add some of that termite nest to get rid of these mosquitoes. They're biting me to bits.'

The lumps of termite nest soon began to burn freely, and the smoke billowed out in clumps. As Peter had pointed out, the nest was made of termite poo – basically digested fragments of tree, still dry from being in his bag. And it smelled like termite poo! Warmth began to radiate out from the fire and Peter huddled closer.

'Take your shoes and socks off,' Beck told him. 'We need to get them as dry as we can.'

The night before, they had roasted lizard tail on a spit over a fire. This time the spit held their footwear, suspended over the low flames. It was never going to be a roaring bonfire, but given the small size of their treetop camp, that was just as well.

CHAPTER 23

By now the rain had stopped and darkness had fallen. Neither boy felt much like chatting. They sat quietly and enjoyed a dinner of figs and bananas and the grubs they had collected during the day. Some of these were large enough to be roasted on the end of twigs. They washed down their meal with water from the bamboo sections. It wasn't as filling as the lizard they'd eaten the night before but it would do until morning.

And they listened to the jungle. Up here, halfway between the ground and the canopy, there was a new layer of sound. The animals calling to each other felt closer, more immediate. Their ears seemed to pick up new frequencies that they just didn't catch down below.

And then they heard a sound that made them very glad they weren't down below. A bass rumble, a snarl, a sound like tearing paper and thunder.

Their eyes met. Peter's were wide.

'Tiger,' Beck said softly. He peered over the edge of the nest. By now the floor of the jungle was swathed in gloom and he couldn't see anything. Tigers were adapted to blend in – that was the point of camouflage.

'Does he know we're here?' Peter whispered.

'Maybe. Don't worry. They don't climb trees.'

'So they don't climb and they do like water. Has anyone told them they're meant to be cats?'

There was another roar from below, though they couldn't tell how close it was. The entire jungle seemed to amplify the sound; it echoed all around.

And this time the roar was answered by another animal noise. A hoot and a squawk from nearby – up in the trees, on the same level as the boys. They recognized the sound. It was an orang-utan, very close by.

It was immediately answered by another call behind them. Their heads whipped round.

Something strange was happening. The moon had come up above the canopy, and silver light filtered down through the trees. The humid air turned into a mist that glowed faintly. Branches and leaves were silhouetted as dark lines against it. And it picked out other things too: dark clumps that were other nests; long-armed forms that swung through the leaves as easily as the boys would cross a road.

They hadn't noticed earlier that their nest was part of a small community scattered over a hundred square metres of treetops.

More orang-utan calls, from in front and behind and all around. Beck realized, with awe, that they were communicating. He could imagine what they were saying:

Look out! Tiger spotted in sector seven!

Yeah, don't worry. We've seen it.

Stupid cat.

How's the wife and kids?

Oh, and a big hello to our new friends in number twelve! Glad you could join us.

Leaves and branches rustled loudly overhead. Something heavy was coming their way. They ducked, and an orang-utan swung over their heads. Without even stopping, it grabbed a handful of figs with its free hand and kept going. However, it glanced back and Beck was sure their eyes met. It seemed to give its approval to their staying the night.

'This is unearthly,' Peter whispered. He looked at Beck and his eyes seemed to shine, even in the dark. 'We came to see them in a sanctuary and now we're living among them!'

'Let's hope not permanently, though,' Beck said quickly. 'It's pretty amazing, but we've got a mission – and that is to get our backsides back to safety.'

'We will, Beck. We've done it before and we can do it again.' Peter snuggled down and curled himself into a ball. If that tiger hung around, then they were staying up here for as long as it took, he thought. But there was no doubt that the jungle had given them a blessing he hardly felt they deserved.

'Hope I don't fall out,' Peter mumbled sleepily.

'You won't. They build these things properly.'

There was no answer, and Beck knew his friend was already asleep. He wondered if this was how baby Hannah could drop off so quickly in her parents' arms. She felt safe, secure and watched over. What could go wrong? He lay back, feeling safe and awed while the orang-utans continued to chirp and hoot around them. It was a very bizarre lullaby that soothed him to sleep.

It must have happened very quickly, because before he knew it he was awake and the sun had come up. The chorus of orang-utans had stopped and Peter was whispering his name hoarsely.

'Beck! *Beck!*'

Beck lazily opened one eye. Peter was lying absolutely still, quite rigid, clearly terrified. A hairy tarantula, fifteen centimetres across, was crawling slowly across his chest.

CHAPTER 24

'Don't move an inch, Peter.'

Beck scrambled quickly to his knees and leaned close to study the creature. Body and legs were covered in what looked like thick fur, creamy white with black stripes at the knees and joints. The tarantula seemed to be in no hurry. Perhaps it was wondering what the strange vibrations under its feet were – Peter's rapid breathing and pounding heart.

'Wow,' Beck murmured. 'That's a beauty.'

'Get it off me,' Peter hissed.

'You know how these things eat?' Beck asked conversationally. 'They inject their victim with a venom that liquidizes their insides. Then they just kind of suck it all out—'

'*Get it off me!*' Peter was almost screaming.

'But that's only small animals. Humans are too big.' Beck carefully reached for a stick and the glass knife. 'You know, hardly anyone ever dies of a tarantula bite . . .'

With one swift movement he flipped the spider off his friend and onto the tree. Then he pinned it down and cut off its head.

'Thanks!' Peter snapped. 'No hurry, then! And I *so* wanted to hear all about its eating habits.'

'The nastiest parts of a tarantula are the tiny hairs all over its body and legs,' Beck added. 'They're called urticating hairs – if threatened, the tarantula sheds them and they irritate any predator, getting in their lungs and stuff. It's easy to remember urticating, because if you get them in you, they 'urt!'

'That's a terrible joke, Beck!'

'Anyway, relax. It wasn't going to bite you. Wrong place, wrong time, that's all.' Beck held the tarantula up by one of its feet, using two small twigs as chopsticks. 'But right place and right time for breakfast!'

Peter pulled a face and muttered something under his breath about how Beck should never start a restaurant.

They pulled on their shoes and socks, which were still a little damp but much drier than yesterday. Beck turned his attention to the fire, which was still smouldering. He added a little more termite nest to get a flame going again; then he held up the dead spider.

'So how do we get rid of the hairs? You can't just bite into that!' Peter said, prodding the tarantula.

Beck brushed the spider's body very gently with the tip of the knife. The hairs were barbed and designed to come off and embed themselves in anything that attacked it. 'They aren't lethal but they're incredibly itchy,' Beck replied. 'If they get into soft, sensitive skin, like your mouth, they burn like crazy.'

'So we shave it?'

'No, we burn the hairs off.'

Beck cut the legs off the body and flicked them away with the knife tip. Then he stuck the knife into the seeping hole where the head had been and held the body gently to the flame. He turned his wrist slowly, letting the flame play over every part of the body. It wasn't enough to cook it, but bit by bit the hairs withered and curled and smoked away.

Eventually all that was left was a faint layer of sooty ash which he could brush away with his fingers.

'*Now* we eat it!'

Beck carefully sawed the spider in half. Green and yellow innards oozed up over the glass blade.

Peter groaned. 'Urk. That's the most disgusting thing I've seen *ever*.'

'What, including the scorpions?' Beck asked mischievously. In the Sahara, they had eaten scorpions that looked pretty similar inside.

'I reckon so,' Peter grunted.

Beck used his fingers and the blade to push the innards back in again so that each boy got about half. He wasn't particularly looking forward to this either. When you ate a grub or a termite, it was whole; you couldn't see the insides and could pretend they weren't there. But in this case the spider's innards were on display for all to see and they didn't look good.

He handed Peter his portion. 'On the count of three,' he said. 'One, two . . .'

They popped their spider halves into their mouths. It was pretty much as Beck had expected.

Salty slime – as if he had just coughed up a mouthful of phlegm and it was crawling around inside his mouth. The spider's body was chewy and tasteless, and bits got between his teeth.

Peter had to gulp several times to get his half down, but he managed it in the end. They followed it with more grubs, and then finished off the water from the bamboo sections. It was a meal, but it wasn't a satisfying one.

'Yum,' Peter croaked. 'Full English brekka.'

Beck made himself smile, though at the words *full English brekka* he felt his stomach clench, as if tying itself in knots. That would be one treat he would definitely reward himself with if they got out of here.

Beck grabbed a couple of bananas and threw one at Peter. 'This will get rid of the taste of tarantula!'

They ate their bananas reverently, enjoying their last moment of peace before the struggle began again.

Peter peered out into the trees. 'I think the neighbours have all moved on,' he said.

'Yup.' Beck followed his gaze. For a moment the memory hung in the air – that magic time when they were part of the orang-utan community. Then it was gone, replaced by the here and now. 'And we should move on too.'

'And, um, what about kitty?'

'Ah. Yes.' Beck craned his neck to look down. This time he could see the ground clearly and there was no sign of a tiger. He suspected that a tiger wouldn't bother lying in wait. If there was one down there, with the scent of humans in its nostrils, it would be right at the bottom of the tree, waiting for them.

'He's moved on too. Come on.'

Even the short distance to the ground made a difference to the temperature – as if someone had turned up the thermostat. The air was instantly warmer and more humid, like a wet blanket draped over them. Beck was pleased to see that Peter looked more awake, more alert and with it this morning. It was their third day in the jungle and he seemed to be getting used to the climate.

Back on the ground they could stretch and twist and pace about. The leaf bucket had done its job and they could refill their water bottles. A sudden rumbling noise made Beck glance at Peter. But it wasn't the weather, it was his friend's stomach. Peter wasn't the kind to moan, but Beck knew they needed more food.

'Let's go.'

CHAPTER 25

Like the day before, they walked close to the river but not too close. The lesson of the crocodile was still fresh in their minds.

After a couple of hours the undergrowth became so dense that they were pushed away from the river. Beck kept going in the direction he judged the river had been flowing, heading downhill.

And then suddenly, without warning, the trees cleared and they stumbled straight into an opening in the jungle.

'Cool!' Beck exclaimed in delight.

'*Wow!*' Peter breathed.

The clearing was filled with a deep, wide pool of cool bright water. It was astonishingly blue, as if a child had drawn it and enthusiastically used up all the blue crayon. The sight was almost as refreshing as a plunge into the water itself.

'It's an old volcanic crater,' Beck realized. 'Don't worry – it's so old it's not going to blow.' He and Peter hurried down towards it. 'It's the volcanic minerals that make the water that colour. They're fresh, they're full of fish and they're croc-free.' Beck started to undo his shirt excitedly. 'This is going to be heaven!'

Peter held back. 'How do you know it's croc-free?' he asked. 'The one we saw was pretty well hidden.'

Beck gestured at the crystal-clear water. 'You'd see one if it was hiding. The water's too clean. They prefer rivers, where the water's murkier. This isn't part of the river, it just fills up with rainwater. And look . . .' He pointed towards the other side of the pool. A couple of small gibbons were crouching by the edge, drinking the water from cupped hands. They had grey fur, their faces ringed with dark bands. The pair had noticed the two boys and were watching them suspiciously. But as long as there was a pool between them, they seemed happy.

'I think they'd have noticed if there was a croc lurking. Or the croc would have noticed them.' Beck kicked off his shoes. 'C'mon!' He ran forward in his shorts and dived in gracefully, hardly disturbing the water.

It was like plunging into cool, liquid silk. Water rushed and gurgled in his ears. It gently washed away the sweat and grime of the jungle and left his skin tingling. He felt the scab on his arm crack and dissolve beneath the bandage. Beck opened his eyes. The world was blue and hazy. The depths grew darker and he could see the outlines of submerged branches, crooked and twisted at the bottom. Sunlight was a rippling shimmer above. And then a much smaller streamlined shape flashed past his eyes and his thoughts latched onto a new thought. Fish! *Food!*

There was a muffled explosion in his ears and a shape plunged past him in a cloud of bubbles. Beck came up to the surface and watched Peter streak across the pool like a small torpedo. His friend had overcome his worries about crocodiles: he was doing the crawl, the stroke that had helped him win swimming prizes back home. Arms and feet churned the water into white foam. The gibbons took one look and fled.

Beck swam around for five minutes before returning to the bank, where their clothes were lying in discarded piles. So, he thought, how to catch some fish? You needed bait, and you needed something to catch them with.

He mulled it over for a few seconds, and then his attention was caught by a brown bulge on a nearby tree. It was another termite nest. Well, that was the bait problem solved.

While Peter continued to cruise around the pool, Beck cut a couple of lengths of rattan vine, each one about a metre long. Then he picked up his trousers and threaded the vine through the belt loops. The vine was flexible but it didn't bend too much, and that kept it firm. The result was a loop that held the waist of his trousers open, as if they were being worn by an invisible man.

While Beck waited for Peter to rejoin him, he did the same for his friend's trousers. Then he tied the legs into knots.

'Proper heaven!' Peter emerged from the pool dripping and grinning. 'Whatcha doin'?'

'We're gonna catch fish.' There were a couple of long, drooping branches that stuck out over the water. Beck pointed at the nearest one. 'Think you can hang off that without falling in?'

He explained what they were going to do as he cut up some liana vine. This was more flexible than rattan and better for using as rope. He cut one length for himself and another for Peter. Then they each tied the ends of their pieces to the belt loops on either side of their trousers. Now they had effectively turned their trousers into cloth buckets, each with a handle.

Beck went back to the termite nest and plunged the knife in deep. Clumps of termites dropped straight out and swarmed over his fingers. He passed a handful to Peter and took another for himself.

The hardest part was crawling out on the branches over the pool. In one hand each boy held a handful of termites; in the other he held his trousers. It didn't free up much for holding on. Beck managed it by leaning forward, clutching the branch

171

with his knees and elbows, and inching forward. Peter copied him, a bit more clumsily but managing to hold on.

They chose branches almost on opposite sides of the pool. If one of them scared the fish off, hopefully they would go straight to the other side.

When they were far enough out, they dropped their trousers into the water by the vine handles. At first the improvised buckets just floated on the surface, but eventually the waterlogged material grudgingly sank beneath the surface.

'Now pull it up until it's just under the surface,' Beck called. 'A few centimetres, no more. And give it some bait . . .'

He sprinkled a few termites onto the water above his sunken trousers. The little insects speckled the surface like confetti and wriggled about indignantly.

Wriggle away, Beck thought. *Lots of nice movement. Let the fish know you're small and edible and not dangerous . . .*

And now it was just a waiting game.

Neither boy spoke as they concentrated on the clear blue depths beneath them. Perched out on their long-limbed branches, there was no shelter from the sun. Beck felt himself slowly bake, and the sparkling water below him made him incredibly thirsty as well as hungry. But he had to be patient.

It wasn't hard to see the fish from up here. They looked streamlined and graceful as they emerged from the dark depths. The boys' splashing about would have driven them down, away from predators, but now they sensed that life in their pool was back to normal. And here were some nice tasty insects that had foolishly crash-landed on their water. But the fish were in no hurry. They weren't starving. They were as happy as their little fishy brains could be.

Beck shifted uncomfortably. The rough wood of the branch dug into places he didn't like anything digging into. The sun beat down on the pool and gently roasted the back of his neck. His arm ached and he wanted to re-bandage it. But there was food down there and they had to get it . . . And just then, it happened.

'Whoa! I'm in!'

CHAPTER 26

Peter sat up suddenly and hauled in on his improvised fishing net. Water drained noisily back into the pool from his trousers. Even from a distance Beck could see the cloth shake as something inside thrashed about.

'Go, Pete!' he called. 'Well done!'

'Uh . . . what do I do with them now?'

'You need to . . .' Beck registered the exact words Peter had used. '*Them?* How many?'

'Two. That's two for me, none for you!' Peter joked.

It took another ten minutes for a fish to take Beck's bait. His patience was wearing thin. Meanwhile Peter had left his two fish on the bank and gone back for another go. Beck caught his one, and Peter caught his third, almost at the same time.

'Two each!' Peter said when they met back on the bank, both grinning wide with triumph. 'Almost as good as eating palm grubs!'

'Yeah, when you don't have any insects to eat, sometimes you just have to make do with roast fish.'

Beck had eaten fish raw before, and it was a tempting thought this time too, as he was so hungry. But apart from a few insects the night before, they hadn't had proper cooked food in over a day. They could do with the energy.

Peter got a fire going while Beck cleaned and gutted the fish. He held them securely, with finger and thumb in the gills – the only way to get a grip on their slithery bodies. Then he cut off their heads. Very gently he sliced all the way down their fronts, taking care not to puncture the guts. After that he could just stick a finger in and hook it round the insides. They seemed to squirm round his finger like worms, and came out like a load of slimy string all twisted together.

The boys roasted the fish over the fire. The rumblings in their stomachs were almost as loud as the snapping of the burning wood. While the fish cooked, they used the time to check Beck's arm and change the bandage again. The gash was still sore but it had clotted over. It didn't seem to be doing much healing beneath the clot, though. It only took the slightest knock to start the bleeding again. Beck knew the only way it was going to heal for good was if he let the arm rest for a few days. That wasn't going to happen until they were back in civilization.

Then they ate the fish. The flavours of the hot juices were the most delicious thing they could remember tasting. Ever. Beck knew it was a good sign when Peter burped.

They had dried off from their swim in the warm air. Now they dipped their hands and heads into the pool's blue waters again, and filled up their bottles. Beck swung his pack onto his back.

'So, which way?' asked Peter.

'Same as before. We follow the river towards the coast – but we don't get too close to the bank.'

Peter stood up and gazed around the clearing. 'Uh, Beck . . . which way did we come from?'

Beck followed his gaze. The edge of the clearing was just jungle, all the way round. There wasn't an obvious path. There were no obvious landmarks. However, he'd made sure to take note of where they'd entered the clearing.

'It's that way,' he told Peter, pointing.

They bade the pool a final reluctant farewell and pushed back into the jungle.

Within five minutes they heard the sound of running water again and were soon back on the river bank. The river had cut itself a little canyon in the floor of the jungle. The sides were three or four metres high, and the river tumbled over rocks and ledges. There wouldn't be any crocs down there, and even if there were, they wouldn't be able to leap up and get the boys. They exchanged pleased looks, and without saying anything they turned to follow the course of the river.

For a few hours they made good progress. They were energized after their hot meal. Drinking was more important than eating, though; it wasn't long before their bottles were empty, but they could always refill them easily.

On one occasion they paused to refill their bottles where a stream cut across their path. To their right it fell down into the river in a two-metre-high waterfall. It was a wonderful sound.

Suddenly a deeper mechanical growl cut through the noise of the water. The boys looked at each other and hope danced in their hearts.

'That sounded like an engine!'

'I think it was.' Beck peered into the trees but there was no way to see through them yet. 'We must be close to civilization.'

Peter's smile split his face. 'Think they'll have a phone? Or a radio? We could call Mum and Dad, and—'

Beck held up a hand as a sign for quiet, then strained his ears. The noise had already died away. Then it started up again for a couple of seconds, and once more died down. For a third time it started up, and this time it persisted. A high-pitched revving that went on and on and on.

'That's not a car,' Peter said, puzzled.

'No,' Beck replied grimly. He thought he recognized the sound and it was not good news. 'Keep quiet and come this way.'

They moved cautiously forward through the

trees, and before long they saw movement. Beck waved Peter down low and they crouched behind a bush.

A scar of cleared land slashed its way through the jungle. The ground was dotted with severed tree stumps. There was a group of five men ahead at the end of the scar, laughing and chatting in Malay. One of them had a radio that was churning out Indonesian pop music. A dirty flatbed truck was parked behind them.

Each man was stripped to the waist, but they all wore safety helmets and goggles, and each was carrying a chainsaw. That was the source of the noise the boys had heard. As they watched, one of the men held his spinning blade to the trunk of a tree, and sawdust spewed out as if the tree were gushing blood.

The other men yanked on the starter cords of their own saws, which joined in the noise. Five dirty petrol-driven saws spewed out a harsh, throaty noise that drowned out the natural rhythm of the jungle.

Cold fury seized Beck's heart. There would be no help from these people, he realized. This was a logging operation, and it was about as illegal as it got.

CHAPTER 27

'They can't do this!' Peter's whisper was outraged. 'This is a protected area. Orang-utans live here!'

Nakula had set it out for them quite plainly. Orang-utans lived in trees; trees got cut down; orang-utans had nowhere to go and died. Beck also remembered what the keeper had told them about the other problems. The damage to the environment, the erosion, the knock-on effects.

Both boys already knew it in their heads. But seeing it was something else. It was the difference between reading about an assault and then seeing someone get mugged in the street in front of them.

'I don't think they care . . .' Beck murmured. But he knew Peter was right, and that just made him even more determined that these men weren't going to see them. How difficult would it be for a group of grown men to 'lose' two boys in the jungle so that no one ever saw them again?

He peered up and down the cleared area. It wasn't large. They hadn't been working that long – probably not more than a day or so.

'They'll be taking advantage of the volcano erupting, I'm sure.'

'Yeah,' Peter whispered. 'They know the police will be too busy clearing up to bother them.'

The fury inside Beck burned even more brightly. He thought of the contrast between these bandits and Nakula, who had dedicated his life to protecting the jungle and had died trying to save the boys. The volcano had killed the kind keeper and probably wrecked many more lives, but these people just took it as an opportunity for crime.

The noise of the saws was deafening. That was good because it meant the boys weren't likely to be overheard. It was also bad, Beck realized, because they wouldn't be doing this if there was anyone else close by. They must still be a long way from civilization.

Peter was shrugging off his pack. 'I'm going to take some pictures. We're going to get back to Medan and we're going to make sure people see these—'

Beck laid a hand on his arm to calm him down. 'Not yet.'

'Not yet?' Peter squeaked indignantly. 'They're destroying the jungle!'

Beck didn't remind his friend of the fact that his camera, or his determination to use it, had got them into trouble once before.

Then the boys froze. The nearest man had cut his saw's engine and laid it down on the ground. He took off his helmet and wiped his brow, then leaned back against a tree trunk and swigged from a can of beer. He was only about five metres away from them.

Eventually the man finished his drink. He picked up his saw and went back to attacking the tree.

Beck put his mouth close to Peter's ear. 'People's minds are programmed to notice human faces,' he murmured. 'They're all basically the same shape and we can pick them out from any kind of background.

183

If that guy just glanced in our direction, he'd see us. So . . . look . . .'

He gestured very carefully at the scar the men had left in the jungle. 'If we make our way round over there, we'll be a safe distance away and they'll have their backs to us. Then you'll be able to use the zoom to get some good pictures. Plus, you can get a shot of the truck's number plate from that angle. That should help the police. Right?'

'Right.' Peter nodded vigorously.

'So follow me. And step super-carefully through all the bushes and branches. One tiny movement down here on the ground can make something really wave about a couple of metres up. Ready? Let's go.'

CHAPTER 28

When Beck had stayed at a village in Borneo, his hosts had an annual tradition of recreating a battle against a neighbouring community. It had taken place a couple of centuries ago but they were proud of their victory. It had been a sneak attack through the jungle, carefully avoiding the enemy's sentries, and Beck's present-day hosts had taught him all the tricks they had used. Hence the crash course he had just given Peter in staying unobserved.

It wasn't just the human face that was easy to make out. The whole human figure is familiar to human eyes. People are born able to recognize it. To be really successful at hiding you needed camouflage: mud on the face to break up the natural lines; leaves or branches to distort the basic human shape.

The boys didn't have time for a full-blown camouflage spree, and they didn't really need it. The men weren't expecting them and they were looking the wrong way. With a little basic care there was no reason anyone should spot them.

Beck led Peter back the way they had come to put a safe distance between themselves and the loggers. Soon they could no longer see anyone, though they could judge their position from the noise of the saws.

Then they made their way round in a large circle, keeping the noise always on their left. On this side of the clearing, if they had to run, they would be running back towards the river. If they had gone round the other side, then they would have had to run deeper into the jungle, away from the river, which Beck didn't want to do.

Beck felt adrenalin course through him as they crept through the undergrowth. It was a nervous charge of energy that turned each of his senses up to maximum. Every leaf stood out in glowing colour; the shrill of every bird and the movement of every insect was magnified. Every scent in the air – rotting leaves, damp mud, ingrained sweat – came alive to his nostrils. He felt primed.

Ten minutes later, as Beck had planned, they were on the edge of the clear area that the loggers had cut. The men were thirty metres away.

Peter already had his camera out. He was the expert, so Beck let him creep forward to the edge of the undergrowth. His face was grim as he zoomed in and began to take picture after picture. Wide-angle shots that took in the whole scene. Close-ups of each of the men, showing their faces where possible. A couple of snaps of the truck, including the number plate as Beck had suggested.

It only took a minute to get a good pile of evidence to put in front of any policeman they met. Peter switched off his camera and put it back in its waterproof case. Then he gave a grim nod to Beck: *I'm finished*. Beck nodded back and they quietly withdrew.

The sound of the chainsaws was muted through the trees. They couldn't see the men any more. Beck judged it was safe to stand up straight and start walking again.

Peter turned, caught his foot on a vine and went headlong. He landed in a tangle of green under-growth with his face in a large red flower. Beck caught his breath and clenched his teeth.

The flower was almost a metre across. Five large petals surrounded a central hollow ball. They were red but flecked with yellow specks, smooth and rub-bery like a giant mushroom.

And it *stank*.

'*Eeuagh!*'

Peter scrambled away from it as quickly as he could. His face was twisted in disgust as he pawed at it to remove every particle of the plant.

'That is *disgusting*!'

It was worse than a pile of Hannah's nappies left out in the midday sun. Beck had recognized it just by sight. It was a Rafflesia – or, as the locals called it, a corpse flower. It attracted insects by looking, and smelling, like rotting flesh. And it was probably the most disgusting smell in the entire world.

'Here . . .' Beck had to fight back a smile as he reached for a bottle for Peter to use to wash the stench off his hands.

When they'd finished, the boys realized they couldn't hear the chainsaws any more. The men were obviously taking a break. Peter's outburst had come at just the wrong time – had they been heard?

Urgent, angry male voices came through the trees, and they were aware of people pushing their way through the undergrowth.

Peter and Beck turned and ran.

There was no time for hiding or camouflaging themselves now. All they could do was put some distance between themselves and their pursuers. It was a straightforward race, driven by desperation. The losers would either go to jail or end up dead.

Vines and twigs lashed at their faces. Fallen branches twisted and moved underfoot. The jungle seemed to be against them, as if it wanted to hold them back and deliver them into the hands of the men who were ruining it. Beck had no idea of direction and no plan for hiding or evading.

The shouts behind them grew fainter, but there was still someone coming after them. It sounded like just one man. One very determined man – which also made him dangerous.

A wall of thorns loomed in front of them. Even as they ran towards it, Beck was scanning it, trying to work out a weak spot where they could squeeze through. But there wasn't one. The vegetation was impenetrable. He cursed under his breath. They were going to have to go round it, left or right. And he could hear the man getting closer and closer, and—

And suddenly every one of his worries became secondary. The hunter chasing them was nothing compared to the hunter that Beck suddenly saw poised on a fallen trunk just off to his side.

The tiger's yellow eyes glared at them. It dug its claws into the tree and bared its long teeth . . . and roared.

CHAPTER 29

Its stripes made it part of the light and shadow of the background. The jungle seemed to shift and shimmer for a moment, then there it was, two metres and 130 kilos of muscle. It felt like the avenging spirit of the rainforest, come to punish the wrongdoers who'd invaded it.

Peter stood paralysed, like a rabbit caught in the headlights. Beck's mind raced: blurred images of a thousand different survival scenarios flashed through his mind in a second. He couldn't latch onto a single one. Fear was winning the mental battle to find a strategy. He fought to control the panic. What to do when a tiger is facing you? Maybe there wasn't anything he *could* do. Maybe that was the point. His mind was working better now. *Just stay still*, he told himself.

The noise of someone crashing though the jungle behind them made Beck look round. The logger! He was the least of their worries now. Beck tried to swallow, clear his throat, shout a warning. But his body wouldn't obey him. It felt like some force was compelling him to keep quiet.

Then he remembered that tigers like to attack from behind. He whipped his head back to face the animal. That was one thing he did know about encountering a tiger – try to keep facing it. This one didn't seem very impressed by the show of resistance. It snarled and lashed its tail.

The tiger's face was narrow. The deep fur around its eyes was striped white and black. Beck suddenly felt he was looking into the eyes of an old, wise man. They were golden, he saw now, not just yellow, and the tiger's gaze seemed to bore into his skull. And Beck suddenly felt goose pimples up his back. He felt their minds connect.

You invade my realm. You take what isn't yours. You bring fire and axes and machines to destroy and despoil.

No! I take only what I need. I eat to stay alive. I

make no mark on your jungle. I respect your jungle. Totally.

And through all his terror, Beck felt such respect for the tiger. It was an amazing creature. A perfect killing machine. Every particle of it belonged in this humid, overgrown world. It didn't matter how hard Beck and Peter tried, they would always be strangers here. Maybe the tiger was the jungle's defence mechanism, the same way Beck's body would produce antibodies if he caught a cold. Maybe this was how the jungle fought back.

Never turn and run . . . Beck remembered now. His father had often told him how tigers are chase animals. They pursue you if you try to outrun them. *Hold your ground. Hold your nerve.* Beck's father's voice was loud and calm in his ear, as it had always been at critical moments in his life. *Hold your nerve.* Somehow Beck felt calm now; he just knew that whatever was about to happen was *right* and they couldn't fight it.

Then the tiger pounced and the spell was broken. A deadly predator was flying straight at them. Beck instinctively dived and pushed Peter away with all his strength, then scrambled away in the other direction. Give it two targets: one of them might survive.

But the tiger reached where they had been standing in one bound, then kept going. It sprang right past them and disappeared into the undergrowth, towards the approaching logger.

Peter and Beck stared at each other.

'It . . . it could have taken us!' Peter gasped.

He was right. It could have. Beck didn't say anything out loud, but he looked back in the direction the tiger had gone for a moment. Did the creature really understand they weren't the ones who were a danger to the jungle?

'Let's not wait for it to change its mind . . .'

They ran in the other direction. Beck wasn't even sure what direction it was, except that it was away from the tiger.

The jungle didn't get any easier to run through. Its hands reached out and grabbed at them. It snagged their clothes and caught their feet. *And where do you think you're going?* it seemed to be saying. *Just hold on a moment . . .*

But fear made them press on. For all they knew,

the tiger might change its mind and come after them. It could be gliding effortlessly through the tangled masses of vegetation while they lumbered their way through.

But then they heard another noise in the distance – a human scream. Then it was cut off, as if someone had thrown a switch.

The boys looked at each other and shuddered.

CHAPTER 30

'Will the tiger come back for us?' Peter asked. His chest was heaving.

'Not if it has its kill.'

Beck slowed down and tried to get a grip. They needed some plan or they would just end up walking in circles. He had to get an idea of their direction again – and find a source of drinking water and food. They would need shelter for that night. None of the basic survival requirements had changed. Protection. Rescue. Water. Food. *Just remember the basics, Beck*.

And they had to keep moving. The tiger was unlikely to be alone.

'We need to find the river,' Beck said, 'and keep going.'

They did find the river again. The sound of running water led them to it. The banks were shallower here. The land was flattening out and the river was widening. Beck knew that this meant they must be getting nearer to the sea. He was still counting on the river bringing them either to the coast or to civilization. It looked like at least one of those might be near.

The boys pressed on through the jungle with a new urgency. It had fed them and sheltered them, but it had also made it quite clear that it did not belong to humans. It had a life-force of its own and it certainly wasn't cutting them any slack. So they followed the water, they kept an eye out for crocodiles and they kept moving.

The river began to widen more now, and its flow grew slower. This was definitely a river nearing the end of its course. The water was getting darker and, Beck noticed, the going underfoot was becoming harder.

They had been climbing over fallen trees, or ducking under low-hanging branches. Now there were times when that was all they seemed to do.

'Is it just me,' Peter said eventually as they helped each other clamber over a tangled mat of dead branches, 'or are all these trees growing horizontally?'

'It's the tsunami,' Beck told him grimly. He helped Peter climb back down to the ground. 'Remember? Boxing Day two thousand and four. This giant wave washed over coastlines all around this part of the world. In some places it went inland a mile and it killed over three hundred thousand people. This place would have been under three metres of water.'

But nature bounced back, Beck reflected. Animals, insects and plants carried on regardless. Nature's relentless march. Apart from the fallen trees, there was nothing to tell this had once been a place of death. The thousands of corpses had long since rotted away, or been consumed by crocs.

Peter was quiet for a moment. Then his face brightened. 'But that must mean we're close to the sea!'

'We can't be far,' Beck agreed, and after that there was a spring in their step.

They still couldn't see any further than the nearest

river bend. It was fun to fantasize that after the next corner the trees would suddenly clear and they would be looking out at a golden beach and blue sea. Then they could collapse onto the soft sand and let their exhausted bodies recharge.

After a while, though, a distinct smell began to tickle at Beck's nostrils and he guessed that they wouldn't be seeing the sea soon after all. The sea would be clean and fresh. This was pungent and rotting.

Sure enough, the view did clear as they came round a bend. The trees thinned out and disappeared. The river widened into a pool of dark water that vanished into a tangle of tall green reeds. Beck's heart sank as he looked out over what lay ahead. He had been forewarned by the smell, but the intimidating vista made the spirit drain out of him. He walked forward to the bank, where dark water lapped at his toes.

'It's a swamp,' Peter groaned, 'isn't it?'

'Yup. It's a swamp.'

At least the jungle had given them firm ground to stand on. What lay ahead was a vast expanse of stagnant, stinking black mud and water. Beck knew it could be waist high, or deeper. It loomed in front of them for a width of about twenty metres, the length of a swimming pool. Then, beyond it, a thick mass of two-metre-high reeds grew straight out of the water. They were so closely packed together that they almost looked like blades of grass in a land of giants.

Beck peered in either direction, along the swamp's edge. Maybe they could go round? But, no, he knew the band of swamp could stretch for miles and miles and miles. Meanwhile the sea could only be a few hundred metres away, dead ahead. And they certainly couldn't go back – not into that realm of tigers and illegal loggers.

Rotting vegetation and putrid water. That had been the giveaway smell. Every dead thing in the jungle that got washed away by the river sooner or later ended up here. This was the sewer of the jungle, more decaying matter and disease per square centimetre than anywhere they had been so far. The home of snakes and death. And they were going to have to wade through it.

CHAPTER 31

'Can we swim it?' Peter asked. He was trying to look and sound optimistic. But from the way his face twisted when he looked at the water, Beck knew his friend was hoping for a miracle.

'No,' he said. 'We're going to have to wade through carefully – and I've got to keep it away from my wound. We definitely couldn't swim through the reeds. The only way to get through them is to push. Backwards.'

'Backwards?'

'The edges of those reeds can shred your face and hands. They are razor-sharp. It's easier to push through backwards.'

'Easy to keep going round in circles too, I imagine.' Peter looked thoughtfully at the bed of towering reeds. His mind seemed to be running through the implications of being waist-deep in reeds that were taller than a man. 'We won't be able to see a thing. No landmarks; we'll barely be able to see the sun to navigate by. We could lose all sense of direction.'

'We need a plan,' Beck agreed. 'If we had some other kit I'd make a compass, but we don't.' He sighed. 'We'll just have to keep an eye—'

'What would you need to make a compass?' Peter interrupted him.

'Something that's metal, and very small. And it would have to be iron or steel. Magnetic. Your camera's all plastic and aluminium, so that wouldn't work and—'

'This is steel.' Peter held up his left hand and his watch flashed in the sun.

Beck smiled and shook his head. 'Sorry, Pete. It's still too heavy—'

'Not the watch. This bit.'

Peter unbuckled the watch from his wrist and held it up. It was an old-fashioned leather strap with a buckle at each end. The central part of the buckle was a thin metal pin.

'That's definitely steel?' Beck felt his hopes rising.

'Definitely. It said on the box.'

'Then it's perfect . . .'

Beck pried the pin of the watchstrap free. It was thin, just over a centimetre long. 'This is going to sound weird . . .'

'A lot of what you say sounds weird,' Peter said dolefully, looking at the remains of his watchstrap. He slid it into a pocket of his daysack and zipped it up.

Beck passed him the pin. 'You need to hold it like this, between thumb and forefinger, and just stroke it through your hair. Slowly and gently, over and over again. At least a hundred times.'

Peter's only further comment was to raise his eyebrows. Then he took the pin and started to do as he was told. 'And this magnetizes it?' Stroke, stroke, stroke . . .

'Eventually.'

Anything with iron in it, like steel, could be magnetized. It was a case of making all the atoms line up in the same direction. That could be done by hitting it repeatedly. Or it could be done with an electric current. Or just a field of static electricity.

205

After three days in the jungle, Beck reflected, their hair was filthy. But even unwashed, matted hair generated a slight static charge when something was rubbed through it. By stroking it through his hair, Peter was gently magnetizing the metal pin. And something that was long, thin and magnetized would always point in one direction, like a compass needle – towards the magnetic north pole.

But Beck still needed something to support it. The field would be so weak that almost any resistance would overcome it and stop the needle from pointing. With a stronger magnet he could have dangled it from a string, or a piece of vine. But this tiny little thing would just be blown around by the slightest puff of wind or movement. Some kind of container was needed, and Beck could only think of one.

He looked unhappily at his water bottle. He could cut the end off it, fill it with water and float the needle on that. He would be plus one compass but minus a water bottle, and he really needed that too.

'If we had wire,' Peter said conversationally (stroke, stroke, stroke), 'we could probably connect the pin to my camera's batteries. It wouldn't be much of an electrical current but it would have the same effect—'

'Yes!' Beck exclaimed. 'Brilliant!'

Though it wasn't the camera he was after. While Peter kept stroking, Beck tugged the camera out of its case and removed the lens cap. It was just a piece of plastic that protected the glass of the lens, about five centimetres across and one deep. And it could hold water.

'Um – may I?' Beck remembered to ask, knowing it was Peter's pride and joy.

'Oh, please, be my guest . . .'

Beck laid the lens cap on the ground and carefully half filled it with water. Then he looked around for something that the pin could float on without sinking. A small green leaf did the trick.

'OK, you can stop stroking now . . .'

Beck took the pin and laid it on the leaf that bobbed around in the middle of the lens cap. It spun gently, slowed down, stopped, and drifted over to one side of the cap. He poked it with the tip of the knife. It spun again, stopped, and again drifted to one side while the boys peered down at it. It came to rest in the same position.

'See,' Beck said happily, 'it's always pointing in the same direction! We've got a compass! Now let's go back up the river, back to where the water's clean, and fill our bottles. It'll be something like ninety per cent humidity in the reeds – we're going to get thirsty. And then we'll go for it.'

Ten minutes later, they slid into the watery gunk of the swamp.

At first it felt revolting, but that was just in the mind. Beck tried to tell himself that it was no worse than walking into a muddy river with his clothes on. But the goo felt slimy as it trickled into his shoes, soaked his socks, worked its way up his trousers. He tried to imagine it was clear and blue, like the pool back in the jungle.

Then they started to walk – or rather wade – and the real yuk factor hit them.

They couldn't see the bottom through the black mud but they could feel it. It was a twisted mat of rotten wood and roots and silt. The tsunami had laid down a whole new layer of debris which had sunk to the bottom. It was impossible to get a sense of balance. The boys wobbled and wavered, and several times they nearly tripped. It was like wading through wet cement. Meanwhile the disturbed mud sucked and gurgled, releasing gas and vapours from the rotting matter: it was like sticking your head down a loo.

In no time at all sweat was pouring down their faces. Swarms of flies buzzed around their heads, relentless and aggressive. Beck knew this was truly hell on earth, but he kept his arms above his head, protecting the compass – and his injured arm – and pressed on.

When you're going through hell, keep walking. Beck's father had often quoted Winston Churchill to him as a boy. He'd been one of his father's heroes.

And so they walked. Every step was an effort. First you had to twist your foot free of the swamp's invisible grip. You had to be firm enough to break the suction, gentle enough not to leave your shoe behind. Then you had to find somewhere more or less secure to put your foot down again. It was slow, hard work, and that was just crossing the open swamp to the reeds. The boys were up to their waists in mud and black water, and the man-high reeds loomed above them like a wall. There was no break in it, no obvious way through.

They looked at each other.

'Backwards?' Peter asked.

'Backwards.'

They turned round to face the way they had come, and then started to move backwards into the mass of reeds.

Immediately it was twice as hard. Every step was a struggle: it took longer to lift up their feet, longer to find somewhere to put them down again, and longer because the sheer weight of the reeds was pushing back at them.

'Ow.' Peter hissed and held up his finger. The edge of a reed had sliced along it. Now there was a thin red line, like a paper cut. It wasn't deep but it stung. He pressed down on it.

'That's why we walk backwards,' Beck reminded him. This way, their daysacks were the first thing to meet the reeds and the reeds could slash away all they liked.

The creepiest thing was the way the reeds rose up again once they had passed. Closing off their way back, hiding their escape, shutting them in.

CHAPTER 32

As Peter had predicted, the sun was often hidden from view; there were no landmarks at all. The reeds were too tall. Sometimes big objects under the water got in their way and knocked them off course – a large tree root or rotting trunk – and they had to work their way around it.

Every five minutes they stopped for a drink out of their bottles. A single mouthful, careful not to let any of the swamp water pollute their supply. They used this time to check their bearings as well. Everywhere looked the same, and visibility in any direction was only about two metres, so they were doubly grateful for the compass. Without it they really would have been effectively blind. They would inevitably go round and round in circles until they collapsed with dehydration and exhaustion. Beck clutched the compass tightly.

The depth of the swamp varied. Sometimes the mud only came up to their waists. Sometimes the bottom fell away and it almost reached their shoulders. Beck still had both arms held up, one to keep the compass steady and the other to protect his cut, and his shoulders felt like lead weights. It also made balancing hard, and before long the muscles in his arms were shrieking, but he had no choice but to keep walking.

Peter shuddered as they started to push their way slowly through the sea of reeds again. His gaze darted all around nervously.

One of Beck's main concerns here was snakes. They loved dark, dank swamps, and in the black water the boys couldn't see where they were treading. And Beck was in front. The first to get bitten if he trod on one. But he was powerless to do anything except trust fate and press on.

'That trick you taught me . . .' Peter muttered. 'How to fight claustrophobia? It's not working.'

'Don't think too much, just focus on keeping

moving.' When Beck had taught Peter how to look through the jungle, that had assumed there was something to see. Different kinds of tree, different levels to the terrain. You could get the shape of the jungle around you. But the swamp had no shape. It was just flat, and all you could see after the reeds was more reeds. Their best tactic was just to push on as fast as they could.

Not only was it hot, it was also unnervingly quiet. They had got so used to the background noise of the jungle that they had stopped noticing it – until it was gone. The reeds were perfect sound insulation. Not a single squeak got in from outside. The only sounds came from their shoes squelching in the water and mud. The rustle of reeds around them. And, of course, the maddening buzz of the insects that swarmed around them. It was like being in their own little universe – hot, humid and claustrophobic. Beck wondered if and when there would be an end to this hell-hole.

'If it's any help, swamps are formed near large bodies of water.' It was the only helpful thing he could think of.

'Like the sea?' Peter said hopefully.

'Like the sea. So we can't have that far to go.'

Peter smiled. Beck could see the effort it took and smiled back.

'Then we'd better get on . . .'

Because they couldn't see or hear anything more than a very short distance away, the end came as a surprise.

They had learned to brace themselves against the mass of reeds at their backs. The resistance vanished so suddenly that they fell backwards with shouts of surprise. Beck felt himself falling and his arms windmilled for balance. Everything seemed to slow down. He even had time for a couple of thoughts. Part of him noticed the compass that he had preserved so carefully fly out of his hand. He felt annoyed that the needle would be lost in the depths of the swamp. Another part warned him more urgently that he was falling backwards into the filthy water. It would get on his arm; close over his head.

And then he hit something solid and the breath was knocked out of him.

Time and his thoughts returned to their normal

pace. He was lying on a sandy bank. Only his feet were still in the water. Peter was lying next to him, looking equally surprised; he sat up slowly, pulled his feet out of the swamp, and began to giggle.

'What?' Beck felt a smile tugging at his own lips. The laugh was infectious – fuelled by adrenalin and relief.

'You look filthy, Beck.' Peter fell back onto the sand again, shaking with laughter. Beck looked down at himself, then at Peter, and started to laugh too. From the shoulders down their clothes were stained black and brown, and coated with slime and weed.

In this new world of light and air beyond the smothering embrace of the reeds, Beck's ears picked up the most beautiful, *cleanest* sound ever. The sound of waves hitting the shore.

CHAPTER 33

'Hear that?'

'Way ahead of you!'

The two boys scrambled further up the sandy bank, away from the swamp. They reached the top and gazed out over a sight that could have come out of a holiday brochure. Gentle waves rolled in from a sparkling blue sea onto a shallow slope of golden sand. They curled into tunnels and collapsed in clouds of broken spray.

Both boys whooped and broke into a run. They shook off their packs as they went and ran straight into the sea, keeping going until the waves broke over them. The salt water felt good and healing on Beck's wound.

They emerged from the sea dripping wet but

much cleaner. They would let the sun and sea breeze dry them off. Beck trudged back up the beach to the highest point and looked back the way they had come.

The swamp before him was probably a half-mile across, though it had felt ten times that. Then there was the jungle, rising up in a gentle slope for several miles, looking so serene, so peaceful. Like a carpet of green. But hiding a world of chaos and danger beneath it.

Then, on the horizon, Beck saw something he had almost forgotten about – Lasa, the volcano that had started all this. There was a gentle puff of smoke drifting up from its summit, nothing more. It obviously hadn't been a major eruption. Beck felt a wave of anger stir inside him. That stupid volcano had chosen to blow off a bit, causing the death of poor Nakula and all the trouble since . . .

'Doesn't look much, eh?' Peter murmured, coming to stand beside him.

It was a little dispiriting to see how far they had come. Three days in the jungle when a car on a decent road could have done it in half an hour.

'We did good in there, Peter, but we're not home yet,' Beck said softly, and turned away.

He knew the beach seemed like the answer to their prayers. He also knew it was a false hope. In the jungle the trees had kept in the humidity but they also kept off the sun. Here there was no protection. If they weren't very careful, they could dehydrate and die just as fast in the open.

And they would need water. Their bottles were almost empty. The sea gleamed with cool, blue water they couldn't drink – salt water was a poison that would dehydrate them and drive them mad, destroy their kidneys and ultimately kill them.

We need fresh water, Beck thought. The swamp was fed by a river. Somewhere that water had to find a way out again, or the swamp would just burst. And it didn't take long to find. About a hundred metres away, a wide, shallow river broke through the sand bank and flowed across the beach to the sea. The water was clear and completely free of particles.

'We're going to drink that?' Peter asked, aghast, as Beck filled the bottles. 'We've seen where it's been!'

'Exactly!' Beck screwed the tops back on. 'Reed beds are excellent filter systems. All the grot stays in them and what comes out is way cleaner than what went in. There are places back home – all around the world in fact – that use them instead of sewage works – farms, housing estates, any kind of ecological development. More environmentally friendly, better for biodiversity, no chemicals.'

To make his point, he scooped up a handful of water from the river and drank it. Peter reluctantly followed suit, and pulled a face.

'Cool.'

Beck looked up at the sun, checked his watch, and then looked up and down the beach. They had a few hours of daylight left. But where to go in that time? A good question. So far he had just concentrated on getting out of the jungle. He had followed the river on the grounds that it would either reach civilization or the sea, one or the other. And it had. But now? The beach they had come to was a ribbon of sand between sea and swamp. It could stretch for miles in either direction.

There wasn't a soul in sight, not a hint of which

way might be best to go. Not even a ship out on the horizon. But they needed a direction, a plan. It was important to keep going.

He thought out loud. 'We were south of the road between the volcano and Medan, and we came south-east, so Medan must be to the left. But it might still be miles away and there may be somewhere closer to the right.'

'Toss for it?' Peter asked, and Beck shrugged.

'Why not?'

Peter dug out a coin – one thousand rupiahs. 'Heads right, tails left.' He tossed it, caught it and squinted at the side that was up. 'It's ... um ... some kind of bird.'

'That's the Indonesian coat of arms, and it's heads. So we go right.'

They splashed through the shallow river and carried on down the beach, while the waves kept breaking on their left and the sun beat down hard on their heads.

CHAPTER 34

'Hey, Beck!' Peter called. 'Why did the tide go out?'

They weren't talking much. Walking was hot and thirsty work.

The sea breeze gave the illusion of fresh air, until you realized that your sweat wasn't actually evaporating. They had their sleeves rolled down and shirts done up to protect their skin against the sun. If it weren't for their hats, then their brains would have been frying long ago. Beck was glad they hadn't reached the beach until after midday, when the sun would have been at its highest and hottest.

'I don't know,' Beck answered. 'Why did the tide go out?'

'Because the sea weed!' Peter sniggered and Beck rolled his eyes.

'How old are you? Four?'

'Yeah. Will you carry me, then?'

They kept walking in silence for a while. They stuck as much as possible to the sand that lay below the high-water mark. It was moist and firmer than the dry, loose stuff above. Better for walking on. The line was marked out with dead wood and weed and the occasional piece of manmade rubbish. It was all baked dry by the sun, so they would have no difficulty finding fuel for a fire that night.

Beck carefully studied every bit of flotsam that they came to in case there was something useful. A grimy length of rope, embedded with bits of weed. An old crate, which he could break up for firewood. An empty two-litre plastic bottle that had once held a fizzy drink.

'Might come in handy,' he said, and put it in his pack.

When the afternoon rain came, they stood out in the open under the heaving sky. It was good to be able to wash, and to fill their bottles with fresh rainwater.

But the rain didn't last long. Then it was back to more walking.

'OK, why does the sea roar?' Beck asked eventually.

'Don't know . . .'

'So would you if you had crabs on your bottom!'

Peter snorted. 'How long were you thinking that one up?'

'About an hour.'

'My legs really ache. And this is me talking, not a four-year-old.'

'I know.'

Beck felt it too. The slight slope of the beach meant that their right legs were taking shorter steps than their left, and that made their hips ache. There wasn't much that could be done about it.

A good excuse to rest soon came along. Beck's eyes lit up at what he saw ahead on the beach.

'Fancy a break?' he asked.

The sand between the sea and the high-water mark was dotted with green specks. They were whelk shells – spirals like ice-cream cones the size of a clenched fist. Some of them moved, scuttling along on some journey that only made sense to the inhabitant.

Beck stood over the nearest one and quickly picked it up. Six spindly legs stuck out from beneath the shell, but their owner pulled them in the moment it realized someone had got it.

'Shellfish?' Peter asked.

Beck passed it to Peter, who turned it in his hands as he studied it. It was just possible to make out a brownish-purple crustacean lurking in the depths. 'Hermit crabs. They don't own these shells, they just borrow them. And tonight we're going to eat them.'

Peter's stomach rumbled at the thought. It seemed a very long time since they'd eaten the fish from the pool in the jungle.

He helped Beck gather up every crab they could find. They put them in their packs, zipped them shut and carried on walking.

The end of the day came as quickly as it had in the jungle. Out in the open, they could actually appreciate it. They were on the east coast of Sumatra and the sun sank down in the west, on the other side of the island. Red light scattered across the jungle and the beach, and their shadows stretched down to the sea like those of giants. The sky to the west was streaked with bands of orange and purple. To the east the dark came rushing in at them off the sea.

It only took a few minutes. The colour leached out of their vision and left only black and white and shades of grey. Night time scarcely made a difference to visibility because the moon was up – almost full in a cloudless sky. The boys could still see each other quite clearly and they kept on walking without a break.

And then, very faintly, the wind carried the whisper of a roar.

CHAPTER 35

The roar came from across the swamp, out of the jungle. They had no difficulty recognizing it.

'Um,' Peter said, 'you know you said tigers are nocturnal . . .'

'He's got no reason to cross the swamp,' Beck told him as they trudged on. 'Not when he's got the jungle to himself again. He's just saying goodbye.'

But even though his tone was flippant, they both glanced with respect in the direction of the roar. Beck knew that it might well be the same tiger they had seen. They were solitary animals and patrolled a wide territory.

'It could have killed us,' Peter murmured, 'just like that, but it didn't. We're only alive now because it let us be.'

'So we use that gift,' Beck said.

'To do what?'

'To make sure the authorities hear about those loggers.'

They kept going for another couple of hours, finally calling a halt when the tide came in, forcing them off the firm sand. There was a cluster of coconut trees on the highest point of the beach, between sea and swamp, which Beck thought would make a good campsite.

He wasn't wrong. For a start, there was a slight hollow between the trees that would shelter them from the sea breeze during the night.

'Welcome to Hotel Peter and Beck!' He clambered quickly up the nearest trunk. Long leaves exploded out in all directions at the top of the tree. Beck started to hack away clumps of them, as well as a cluster of coconuts sheltering in their midst. The coconuts hit the sand below with a satisfying *thud* that told him they were full of milk and flesh.

Peter, without even being asked, was building a fire out of the remains of the crate Beck had found earlier. Handfuls of crumbling dry seaweed provided the kindling. Beck jumped down and handed him the fire steel. Peter struck the fire's first sparks and blew gently on the smouldering palm fibres to encourage the flame while Beck arranged the coconut leaves into two mats.

'We're just sleeping on the sand?' Peter asked. He sounded faintly surprised.

'No, we're sleeping on the leaves on the sand. Why?'

'I'd just read about this disease . . . um, leishmaniasis? You get it from sand flies and it gives you *really* nasty sores, so you're supposed to sleep off the sand . . .'

Beck grinned. 'But you don't get it in Southeast Asia. You get it in America, north and south, and Asia, and the Middle East . . . but not here.'

'Wow. You mean, someone somewhere is actually cutting us some kind of break?' The fire had caught nicely with the bone-dry wood. Peter sat down next to his friend and held his hands out to the warmth. 'That's the nicest thing that's ever happened to me.'

'Well, there was not being eaten by the tiger. That was quite cool.'

'OK. Second nicest thing . . .'

They cracked open the crab shells with a rock and killed the crabs with a single blow. Each one of them had a single large claw and Beck showed Peter how to twist it off.

'All the flesh is on the inside, and the claw is the bit with the most of it,' he said. 'And cooking is easy . . .'

Cooking was just throwing the shells into some embers at the side of the fire to cook slowly. That bit really was easy. What was much harder was waiting while the smell of cooked crab tickled their noses and twisted their empty stomachs into knots. But when they finally ate, the taste of cooked food in their mouths was like an explosion of flavour and texture and juices. The wait was so worthwhile.

They used the crowbar to open up a couple of coconuts too. The lukewarm, oily coconut water inside was the perfect dessert.

'It's like being back in the desert again,' Peter commented afterwards. Beck looked up from his work. He was sharpening a pair of sticks into points; the next morning they would use them for fishing.

Peter was lying on his back next to the fire and looking up at the stars. He yawned and stretched; Beck gave him about five minutes before he fell fast asleep. 'Except we're next to the sea, it's not freezing cold at night and no one's had to pee on anyone.'

Beck chuckled. Back in the Sahara, they'd had to wrap damp T-shirts around their heads to protect them from the desert heat – and the way to make the T-shirts damp without wasting water was, yes, to pee on them. He remembered Peter's horrified reaction to that news, and smiled.

'Though the journey's not over yet . . .' Beck pointed out.

But Peter was already asleep.

CHAPTER 36

Beck was standing up to his waist in the sea and staring intently into half an empty plastic bottle. The water surged lazily up and down his body.

It was early in the day but already warm. He had woken with the dawn and left Peter sleeping. He wanted to do this while the sun was still low, because the higher it was the stronger it would get. He had left his clothes on the beach and was only wearing his shorts. He could feel his shoulders already growing warm. Much longer and he would get burned.

He could have just kept his shirt on, but it would only get in the way while he was swimming. The wet fabric would be heavy and slow him down. If he found what he was looking for, he wouldn't need to worry about sunburn while he was in the water. And no one liked wearing wet clothes if they could help it.

Beck always smiled at those movies where the hero dives into water and can see perfectly beneath the surface. He can also stay down for minutes at a time on one breath. Beck knew from experience that if you didn't prepare and train, your lungs felt like they would burst after just a few seconds. And as for seeing perfectly, the best you could do was make out blurred shapes.

And so he had taken the plastic bottle they'd found the day before and cut the top off. This left him with a clear plastic tube, sealed at one end. By pushing this below the surface he got a clear view of life underwater. It was already clear enough for him to make out basic shapes, but this was like having a face mask, except that it wasn't fastened to his face. Now he could see everything.

The sea bed where he stood was sandy and striped with rippling light. Fronds of seaweed grew out of the sand and waved back and forth with the motion of the waves. There was a thin coating of small dark pebbles that had been worn smooth and round by the waves. Further out, Beck had already seen that the floor was rockier and coated with sea-weed of red and blue and green.

A couple of fish flickered past him. They were about thirty centimetres long and they completely ignored him.

'What are you doing?' a voice called.

Peter had woken up and was standing by the water's edge. He had his head on one side, watching Beck quizzically.

Beck held up the bottle. 'Just testing . . .'

His foot had knocked against something solid, and it moved. He quickly pushed the bottle back into the water and gazed through it. A delighted smile spread across his face. 'Perfect!'

From the shore, Peter saw Beck suddenly disappear below the surface. Then he stood up straight again, with water sluicing down his head and shoulders, and waded back to the beach with the bottle in one hand and what looked like a large rock in the other. It was the size of a squashed football, but it was light enough for him to carry easily.

'Coral,' Peter said correctly when Beck got back to shore.

'It's called mushroom coral,' Beck corrected him, 'and it's very cool.'

On one side the lump of coral was rough and knobbly, like a cauliflower. The other side was ribbed with dark lines that did look like the gills of a giant mushroom.

Beck crouched down and held the coral on its side. Sea water trickled out of its nooks and crevices onto the sand. 'Coral isn't rock,' he commented idly as they waited. 'It's an organism. Millions of tiny organisms growing together. The Great Barrier Reef in Australia is hundreds of miles long and it's all one living creature. People think that cutting off chunks of coral isn't a problem. But it *is* a problem. You kill it, bit by bit. Reefs are dying all over the world and they're taking whole marine habitats with them.'

'Yet here you are, with a lump of coral . . .' Peter pointed out.

The trickle of water was dwindling. Beck looked up briefly and grinned before concentrating on the lump again.

'Mushroom coral grows in lumps like this. It never gets much bigger. This is the whole thing. It rolls around, loose, in the surf. And when the tide goes out, it gets stranded in the sunlight.'

'Must need some powerful sunblock, then,' Peter commented, smiling. He squinted up at the sky without enthusiasm. When they were in the Sahara, sunstroke had almost killed him as his body overheated.

'That is exactly what it has.'

'*What?*'

'It has a natural sunblock. Look.'

Beck poked the bottom end of the coral. Now that the water had drained away, a slimy mucus was pooling in its place.

'It generates its own type of sunscreen,' Beck explained. 'Factor fifty, at least! And the great thing is, it doesn't hurt the coral at all. We'll rub this on ourselves and then put it back in the sea. Everyone's happy. Here, hold it for me, will you?'

And he matched actions to words. Peter held the coral while Beck caught the dripping mucus in his cupped hands. Then he rubbed it onto his shoulders and up and down his arms and face. After that, Beck held the coral while Peter did the same.

Now that they could walk around in the sun without getting the skin burned off their backs by the sun's rays, they went fishing.

They stood out in the sea at waist depth, about ten metres apart, with the sticks Beck had sharpened the previous night.

'So we don't use the bottle, then?' Peter called.

'No. There's only one and it would get in the way. We need both hands now. The water's clear enough to see if a fish comes near us. We can make out the shape, but remember the light gets refracted by the water. You assume the fish is right in front of you because we're used to light moving in straight lines. But light gets bent when it hits the water. The fish won't be where it seems to be, it'll be about fifteen centimetres behind. That's where to aim.'

And so they waited, spears poised, eyes scanning the water for the dark, streamlined shapes.

And they waited, and they waited. A couple of times Beck or Peter would lunge. But the fish were playing hard to get.

Beck started to cast glances out to sea, towards the deeper water. There were rocks out there. Maybe there would be more fish there, with all the hiding places and plenty of weed to nibble.

Suddenly he heard a cry of triumph from Peter, who held up his stick with something dripping and dark impaled on the end. It looked like a thick, black, pickled leather sausage, the length of his forearm. Peter's look of glee changed comically to disgust.

'*What* is *that*?'

'Sea cucumber.' Beck bit back a laugh. 'They're edible . . . sort of. Better than nothing. Take it back to shore and keep trying. Oh – and by the way, inside it isn't cucumber, but guts and intestines!'

Peter winced. 'I should have guessed.'

Beck's mind was made up – if all they got was sea cucumbers here, he was going to try the deeper water.

He started to prepare himself for diving into deep water. First he needed some good, strong doses of oxygen. He breathed out . . .

'*Out, out, out!*' The old diver in Borneo who had shown him this trick had pushed his fist hard into the base of Beck's stomach, forcing the breath out of him with a *whoosh* that almost made him faint with surprise. *'All old air, out!'*

Then: *'In, in, in!'* Breath had gushed into the little man's mouth and he had seemed to swell to twice his normal size. Beck had followed suit. Ordinary breathing only used a fraction of the lungs' capacity. With a bit of effort you could use much more.

They repeated the process several times until:

''Nuff, 'nuff, 'nuff! No get the dizzies!'

Beck had been at the early stages of his GCSEs and he roughly understood the science behind this. The old man just knew what worked. Oxygen is a highly reactive and toxic gas. Just the smallest amounts are needed to supply energy to the body. More than that and it actively starts causing damage. Too much oxygen in the blood leads to hyperoxia: that is to say, nausea, cramps or, as a first sign, 'the dizzies'.

But thanks to the old man's training Beck knew when he was ready. A few of those deep breaths charged up his body. He could feel the oxygen tingling in his blood. He took a final breath, held it, and dived down.

Water roared in his ears and he could hear his blood pounding in his skull. His vision was reduced to a few blurred shapes. The salt in the water gnawed away at his eyes like an army of tiny insects, but then the sensation eased. The water was clear and the sun was shining brightly above. It lit everything up. He could make out shapes, tell what was moving and what wasn't. With a few powerful kicks and strokes of his arms he pulled himself down towards the rocks.

He needed the oxygen in his blood down here because he couldn't rely on the gas in his lungs. He was only about two metres down but the weight of the water was already compressing the air in his lungs to half its size. He didn't have long. His eardrums were also feeling the squeeze of the water pressure. Beck pinched his nose and blew gently, equalizing the pressure in his ears. They felt better instantly.

Then something blurred in the corner of his eye. A fish – maybe two or three, maybe a shoal. He couldn't see more clearly than that. He lunged with his spear in that general direction, but didn't get anything.

And now he felt his lungs bursting and it was time to go up again. He kicked himself towards the surface. From habit he held his fist clenched above his head as he went. If you accidentally surfaced under a boat, or another diver, it was better to find out with your hand than with your head. Beck smiled. If only he *had* surfaced under a boat, that would be perfect!

He broke the surface with a splash and breathed in gratefully. Water cascaded down his face and he wiped it out of his eyes. He trod water where he was and looked around. Peter had gone back into the shallows and was stabbing vaguely at anything he saw. He wasn't having much luck. They waved to each other while Beck started on a new course of deep breaths. With practice, his personal best was two minutes under water. He wondered if he could make it up to three.

And then suddenly Peter cried out in pain and collapsed into the water.

CHAPTER 37

'Pete?'

Beck forgot all thoughts of records. He dropped his spear, put his head down and ploughed through the water towards his friend.

By the time he reached the shallows, Peter was sitting up, though his face was screwed up with pain. Beck put his feet down and waded towards him.

'*Aargh!* It *hurts!*' Peter looked miserably up at him. 'I trod on something – don't know what but it *hurts* . . . Think it's still there . . .'

'C'mon, then, let's have a look . . . ?'

Peter sat back and lifted his foot out of the water. Beck winced when he saw what came up with it. A black, spiky ball the size of both fists put together clung to Peter's sole like a little alien. Beck knew better than to touch it.

'Man, you've trod on a sea urchin.'

Urchins are covered in hundreds of needle-thin spines. They're so sharp they just slide into the skin of their victim. But because the spines are barbed, they embed themselves like an arrow and grip the flesh, refusing to let go. That's why they hurt and cause such tissue damage. They are like tiny, lethal, one-way spears.

Peter groaned. 'Are they poisonous?'

'Some are. They can inject a small amount of venom. It won't harm a human – but they do hurt a lot.'

'Yep, I'll testify to that!' Peter replied through gritted teeth.

'Let's get you to the beach.'

Beck helped Peter up onto his good foot, and supported his friend as he hopped through the shallows back to the shore. Peter collapsed onto the sand back at their camp.

'Look on the bright side,' Beck said as he studied the urchin. 'You caught our breakfast. Sausage and eggs!'

'Huh?'

'OK, sea cucumber and urchin eggs . . .' Beck bit his lip to contain a smile. 'This isn't just going to come out, I'm afraid. The spines are barbed and embed themselves into you. I'll have to break them off.'

'Just do it!' Peter gasped.

'Right-oh. The good news . . .' Beck reached gingerly towards the first spine in Peter's foot. Even with just thumb and forefinger, he got several jabs from its neighbours. He twisted and the spine snapped. 'They're made of calcium carbonate, just like our bones. So' – he reached for the next and winced at more jabs: *snap* – 'they just snap off' – he moved on to the next: *snap* – 'and they should just dissolve in the body' – *snap* – 'because they're basically made of the same stuff as our bones, so the body just takes them in. It doesn't try and reject them.'

Every time he snapped one of the spines, he put more pressure on the ones that remained. Peter groaned again.

At last they all broke together and the urchin

body just fell away. Beck had his first clear view of the wound. The spines were a cluster of dark dots in the sole of Peter's foot. Some stuck out by a couple of millimetres, some were lodged deeper beneath the skin. The skin was discoloured, black and purple like a bruise. But Beck knew the colour was harmless – it was only dye from the urchin.

'How does it look?' Peter gasped.

'You'll keep your foot,' Beck said with a straight face. Peter sighed in relief. 'In fact, I've got a nice glass case at home you can keep it in.'

Peter scowled and flung a fistful of sand at him.

'OK, OK.' Beck laughed. 'Right. The shallow spines, the short ones – they'll just dissolve inside you in a few days.'

'And the deeper ones?' Peter asked.

'The deeper ones could need surgery – and no, I'm not going to do the job with a glass knife and a crowbar. You'd need a proper doctor to decide that in the first place . . .'

Beck trailed off and Peter looked at him suspiciously.

'I hate it when you do that because there's always

something you really don't want to tell me!'

Beck sighed. 'We should keep the wound clean and sterile. If we washed it in sterile water, which we don't have, or vinegar, which we don't have, that would do the trick and it would help the spines dissolve.'

'But . . . ?' Peter could tell he wasn't finished.

'But we do have something that's sterile, and liquid, and will help the spines dissolve and probably help with the pain too . . .'

The penny dropped.

'I don't believe it! You're talking about pee, aren't you? Pee *again*? It's not enough that we pee on our T-shirts, now you want me to pee on my foot?'

Beck shrugged. 'Blame nature. Not me.'

Peter propped himself up on his elbows and bent his leg so that he could peer at the spines. 'Well, for a start, I went when I woke up and I haven't got any at the moment. Plus the angle's all impossible. Well, impossible for *me* . . .'

He gazed hopelessly at Beck, who was suddenly finding it very hard not to grin wickedly.

'So when did you last go?' Peter asked.

'Let's just say I believe I could deliver.'

Peter looked as if he was about to protest more, but then he gave up. 'It hurts too much,' he muttered. 'Just do it, will you?'

Beck stood. 'Probably best if you lie on your front . . .'

Peter rolled over. 'Oh, believe me, I *so* do *not* want to watch.'

CHAPTER 38

It was quite possibly the most ridiculous image that Beck could have imagined, and Peter shook his head in the sand, mumbling that this really was the last time he went anywhere with Beck.

Beck tried not to laugh as he peed and kept apologizing to his friend.

'Well, that was about as pleasant as you'd expect when your best friend is peeing on you,' Peter grumbled. He rolled back onto his front and sat up, keeping his injured leg stretched straight out.

'Better your best friend than your worst enemy,' Beck said optimistically. 'And out here that enemy is infection. How does it feel?'

'Wet. And maybe a little less achy. Still bloomin' painful.'

'Well, just stay there, and I'll make breakfast.'

Breakfast wasn't quite the sausage and eggs that Beck had described.

While Peter rubbed himself dry and clumsily got dressed, Beck used the crowbar to bash away the remaining stubs of spines on the urchin. They matted together in a thick mass that he could just brush away. He carefully made a small pile of them where neither of them was likely to tread. Then he drove the sharp end of the crowbar into the shell and it split straight across the middle. Inside was a tangled, gooey mass of guts and sand.

He scooped those out with his fingers. Nestled up against the inside of the shell, he found what he was looking for – a glistening mass of small pinky brown blobs. Those were the eggs of the sea urchin.

Beck put the shell aside and turned his attention to the sea cucumber. Out of the sea it was even more like a large, leathery sausage. Beck slit it open with the glass knife, taking care as usual not to puncture the creature's intestines. Apart from anything else, they could give you a nasty rash. As with the fish back at the pool in the jungle, he could simply hook a finger around the rubbery tubes and pull them out. He spread the sea cucumber out with its mix of red, rubbery flesh and black slimy skin.

'Not much to cook,' Peter said glumly, watching.

'We don't need to cook this. We can just eat it raw. Sushi extreme!'

They ate in silence. The cucumber flesh was salty and rubbery and it felt like they were eating a bicycle's inner tube. The eggs looked disgusting, but went down in a couple of swallows. Fortunately, what they lacked in size and filling power they made up for in boosting energy. Beck felt a lot better and more alert with them inside him.

He looked sideways at Peter, who was gloomily munching on a mouthful of red sea-cucumber flesh. Beck could tell that his friend was pretty down in the dumps. Getting out of there had just become much harder if Peter couldn't walk properly. But Beck knew from experience that when the going got tough, Peter could keep going for ever. Even if it meant walking himself into an early grave. He had come close to doing just that back in the Sahara. But the urchin spines meant Peter was effectively disabled, and Beck suspected they were still hurting a lot more than his friend was going to admit.

Maintaining a positive spirit is a vital part of survival. It doesn't matter how sheltered you are, how much food or water you can find for yourself, if you don't also have the will to keep going, you are already dead. With Peter hurt and in this mood, Beck honestly wasn't sure where to go from here.

'You're thinking about what to do, aren't you?' Peter asked.

'Kind of.'

'So what are the options?'

Beck sighed. 'Option one – I carry you. Piggyback.'

Peter forced a smile. 'That would be fun. What's the heaviest weight you've carried long distance?'

'Much less than you,' Beck admitted.

'So what's option two?'

'Well, I've built a couple of rafts before. Maybe I could do that now. We could paddle along the coast instead.' Beck looked up and down the beach. 'That's if we could get the wood. But even if we did,

I don't know what the currents are like. We could get swept out to sea.'

'Beck,' Peter said patiently, and Beck could hear the pain hidden in his voice, 'there's only one way you're going to cover a decent amount of ground, and that's if you leave me here.'

Beck hadn't even considered that option. 'No. We stick together. That's imperative. We got into this together and we will get out of it together.'

'This beach can't go on for ever!' Peter responded. 'And we've already covered a lot of ground yesterday. I bet that in one day, two maximum, you'd find someone. *Then* you could come back. Meanwhile you leave me with food and water and . . . Well, I'll manage.'

'We don't have two days' worth of food and water to leave with you. The only way is to pick it up as we go.'

'Well, leave me with what we've got.'

'I am not leaving you! OK. I'll carry you. That's decided.'

'You'll collapse in half a day!'

'Half a day's better than nothing—'

Beck held his tongue. He did not want to get into an argument. That could split them apart just as much as leaving Peter on his own.

Everything Peter said made sense, but Beck was still resolved that they would stay together. Whatever the outcome.

He hugged his knees and scowled out to sea so that he didn't have to look at his friend. And that was how he saw the fishing boat, moving slowly along the horizon.

CHAPTER 39

Peter saw it at the same time.

'A boat! Beck, that's a boat!'

Beck thought quickly. The boat was still a long way off. They could shout but they wouldn't be heard.

He looked at the remains of last night's fire. It was a charred pile of ashes and fragments. They hadn't yet got round to making a new one.

'We need to make a signal fire, and quick!'

They scrambled to gather together more wood and leaves.

'Everything,' Beck said. 'Everything we've got – seat stuffing, the lot!'

It took a couple of minutes to pile everything together, but the boat hadn't moved much. It wasn't going fast. Beck tried to work out which way the crew were likely to be looking. Presumably their attention would be on their nets. They wouldn't be looking at the land.

He handed Peter the fire steel. 'Get it going and pile on everything you can think of.'

Then he picked up the largest, longest branch that he could find and began to wave it unevenly and erratically back and forth, desperately trying to catch the fishermen's attention. Behind him he could hear the scraping of the fire steel and Peter's frantic muttering.

'OK, it's going . . .'

Once again the sun-baked wood caught light very quickly. The air above the pile shimmered with the heat. In fact it burned too well. It had a crisp, clear flame and that was exactly what Beck didn't want.

'It's not smoking! We need smoke!'

The edge of the swamp was only a short distance away. The day before, Beck had hoped he would never have to go near it again. Now he ran back to the edge and plunged without thinking into its reeking waters. Clutching the glass knife, he waded over to the nearest clump of reeds and sawed at their bases. The first reed toppled over into the water. He left it floating there and turned his attention to the second, then to the third.

In his mind's eye the fishing boat had suddenly sprouted hydrofoils, or a powerful engine, and even now it was zooming away from the shore, leaving the boys behind . . .

He pulled the cut reeds together in a sodden armful and waded back to the beach. Back at the camp he broke the reeds over his knee, one by one, and dropped them on the fire.

'Eeuw!' Peter choked with disgust and waved his hand in front of his face. The reeds had soaked up the filth of the swamp and now they were releasing it into the air. But they were also sending up billows of thick smoke, a signal that surely even the world's most short-sighted fisherman couldn't miss.

Could he?

Beck couldn't make out details through the glare of sun on sea. Was the boat a little nearer? It was a typical fishing boat that you would see all along this coast – long, thin and slender, with a pointed bow and a sun shelter at the stern.

Were the crew looking towards him?

'Come on! We really need to catch their attention! Can you stand up and help me?'

'I'll damn well try,' said Peter, staggering to his feet.

His good foot was flat on the ground and the other just balanced on the tips of his toes. He stooped, a little crooked, and his face winced in pain.

'Hold your arms up in a Y-shape – like you're dancing "YMCA" but you've forgotten the last three letters.'

Peter obliged. 'What's that do?'

'It's the international signal for distress. It means, *Come and help me!*'

Peter kept his arms up and turned towards the boat. 'I didn't know that. I hope they read the same book you did.'

Beck picked up the branch he had been waving earlier and held it to the fire. The end caught quickly and the fire spread to the leaves. He waved it from side to side again – now a burning brand.

And then he saw that the boat was turning towards them.

CHAPTER 40

'Twenty miles,' Peter said, waking Beck from his slumber.

Miles and miles of beach were chugging slowly past. Beck had been fighting to keep his eyes open but everything was against him. The soft throb of the engine. The rocking of the boat. Above all, the fact that they were *safe*. He didn't have to keep his eyes open for poisonous insects or a source of water. He didn't have to plan ahead for their next meal or where they were going to spend the night . . .

His body had firmly informed his mind, which had been fully keyed up for the last three days, that it was OK to shut down, right now, thank you.

And so it took a moment to realize Peter was saying anything.

'What about it?'

'Twenty miles of beach, I think they're saying.' Peter sat next to Beck, in the shade of the boat's roof. His hurt leg was stretched out in front of him. He gave a nod to the boat's crew of three. They were grinning, friendly Malay men, all wearing hats like lampshades to keep the sun off. One of them was at the rudder; the other two were in the bow repairing a net. Precise movements of their hands made order out of a random, tangled mass of rope.

'They speak Portuguese, which is sort of like Spanish, and I sort of speak Spanish, so we can sort of communicate. And I think they're saying the beach goes on for twenty miles.'

Beck whistled softly to himself. This entire stretch of coast was a thin bar of sand between the swamp and the sea. Sometimes the swamp broke through the barrier and came all the way to the sea. It would have meant that even if the boys had walked this far, they would have had to get through yet more swamp on their own.

'We would have made it,' Beck said quietly. He

cocked an eye at Peter. 'Even if I had been carrying you.'

'Yeah, I know,' Peter said agreeably. 'But aren't you glad you didn't have to?'

'I remember my dad telling me about keeping going. He used to say, *He who sticks it out is he who wins*. It always sounded so clunky, but it always made me smile and think of him. And the weird thing is that he was right, Pete.'

Peter patted Beck's shoulder. It was at times like these that he knew Beck still missed his dad a lot.

'You know, Pete, I feel my parents are around me the most when I am struggling the most.'

Peter replied gently, 'That's because the rest of the time you're too busy living. And that's how it should be, buddy. They are always with you and I reckon they are pretty proud of you at the moment too.'

'Thanks, Pete,' Beck replied. 'Well, together we just kept putting one foot in front of the other, didn't we?'

Peter pulled a face. 'I'm not sure I could even do that – but only because, you know, one foot is basically a giant pin cushion at the moment.'

The fishermen were used to urchins. It went with

the job. They had done a good job of washing and bandaging Peter's hurt foot – no more peeing by anyone, he was glad to see – and they had even managed to get a couple of spines out. Peter pointed out that still left a couple of hundred spines in. This was an exaggeration, but he certainly wouldn't be walking anywhere for a while.

Beck grinned. 'Well, you could,' he said.

'Or crawl.'

'And you would, Pete, knowing you.' Beck grinned. He loved Peter's blind determination.

And like Peter, the boat kept going for another three hours, all the way back to port.

'Port' was a town by the beach. There was no kind of harbour, just dozens more fishing boats pulled up on the sand. The beach was black with nets spread out to dry, and the smell of fish was everywhere.

Beck and one of the fishermen made a cradle with their arms and carried Peter up to where the local police chief was waiting for them. The fishermen had radioed ahead. This man spoke English.

'Peter Grey and Beck Granger? You come this way.'

He led them to the police station, which was a wood and bamboo house under the trees at the edge of the beach. There was no glass in the windows – you just closed the shutters if you wanted to keep the wind out – and a wide veranda gave a good view of the beach. The chief could sit there with a drink and the radio on, and survey his realm.

Beck gathered this wasn't a high-crime area. It was a typical building for an area that was used to typhoons or tsunamis. Brick buildings fell down and hurt people and cost a lot of money to rebuild. Wooden ones like this could be put straight back up.

The chief sat them down on the veranda and told one of his men to bring soft drinks.

'There is all-points alert out for you! They find jeep? Burned out. Whole area burned out – you make right choice to move on. But no burned boy bodies. Everyone say, they get eat by tigers? But' – he nodded at Peter – 'his father say, no, no, Beck Granger look after them both!' The man laughed heartily. 'And Beck Granger here! Beck Granger pretty good!'

'Peter pretty good too,' Beck replied.

CHAPTER 41

'Can I talk to my mum and dad?' Peter asked eagerly. 'Have you got a phone?'

'Of course we have phone. Not primitive.' The chief pushed himself to his feet. 'I bring. You have much tell! Much danger in jungle. Tigers, snakes, crocodiles . . .'

'Loggers . . .' Beck added seriously, and the chief's friendly face grew suddenly very stern.

'Loggers? No logging here! This national park!'

'They were logging,' Beck insisted. 'We saw them.'

Peter patted his daysack. 'Got it on camera too.'

The chief bit his lip thoughtfully, then disappeared inside. When he came back, he was carrying a phone and a laptop.

'I tell you,' he insisted with a grin when he saw the boys' look of surprise, 'not primitive!'

The laptop had a card reader installed in its side. It took just a few minutes to put in the card from Peter's camera, download the pictures and send them off to the regional headquarters.

Peter wasted no more time and called his parents. They were relieved and delighted to hear from him, although his mum was so tearful it took a while to talk any sense. Then they wanted to speak to Beck, but they couldn't because he had already taken the opportunity to be first into the shower.

*   *   *

'It will leave a scar.'

The doctor had arrived by the time Beck re-emerged, fresh and scrubbed clean. He probed the cut on Beck's arm with long, gentle fingers. His English was a little better than the chief's.

'I would have put a stitch in it when it happened,' he said. 'Too late now. You looked after it well.'

'Thank you.'

The doctor wrapped Beck's arm up in a proper

surgical bandage and turned to Peter. 'And now you, young man, with your foot?'

Peter had to sit way back in his chair with his leg stuck out while the doctor examined him.

'Nice dress, by the way,' Peter commented to Beck. The chief's wife had taken Beck's clothes – to wash or maybe just burn after three days in the jungle. She had loaned him a T-shirt and a sarong – a large tube of cloth that wrapped around his waist. It was printed with bright red checks.

'She's got one for you too in a minute,' Beck said as he sat down. 'How's it feel?'

'Still hurts.'

'I can give you something for the pain,' the doctor said, 'but some of those spines went deep. They won't dissolve quickly on their own.'

'Are you going to have to operate to get them out?' Peter didn't look as if he was looking forward to the idea.

'Operate? No. We have other methods.' The doctor stood up and crossed over to the table where he had put his bag.

Beck grinned and Peter's face fell.

'Oh, no. What? Please tell me it doesn't involve peeing . . .'

'It's a little more physical than that.' Beck looked very grave. 'The traditional way is to get a piece of wood . . .'

'Yes . . . ?'

'. . . and they bash the foot with it. Hard. To break up the spines. That way the body can absorb them quicker.'

'*What?*' Peter went pale. 'You're kidding!'

The doctor was fiddling with something in his bag. He didn't turn round. 'Your friend is absolutely right. A very effective traditional method. The only way of getting the spines out . . .'

Peter groaned and let his head fall back. 'This adventure just gets worse and worse.'

'. . . until modern times.' The doctor turned round; he was holding a small syringe. 'Nowadays a simple injection to dissolve the spines has the same effect. It will sting a little, but it's better than being hit with a piece of wood.'

Peter glared at Beck, who felt his straight face crumpling into a big grin. And then Peter started to smile himself, until finally a laugh burst out of him, joining in with Beck and the doctor.

'You know, that's the first time ever I've been glad I don't have to rely on you!'

CHAPTER 42

'Look familiar?'

Peter was still limping a little but he was determined to keep his foot exercised. The doctor had said that this would speed up the process of dissolving the spines. He hobbled over to where Beck, Mr and Mrs Grey and Hannah were having lunch. They sat beneath a large sunshade at the side of the pool on the last day of their holiday.

Peter was holding a copy of the English-language *Jakarta Post*. He laid it down in front of Beck. 'I got it in the lobby . . .'

The main picture on the front page showed armed police surrounding a battered truck. The driver and passengers were climbing from the cab with their hands on their heads. Beck then noticed another picture inset into the main one. It showed the same truck in the middle of a large cleared area of jungle.

'It's your photo!' he exclaimed. 'They used the picture you took to arrest the loggers!'

Peter smiled proudly. His parents scrambled to have a look. Mr Grey read out:

'*Acting on information received from a pair of English tourists—*'

'Tourists?' Beck exclaimed with mock indignation. 'Rugged adventurers, more like!'

'*—armed units of the National Police apprehended a gang of illegal logging criminals on Thursday afternoon. Photographs taken by the tourists helped the police to identify the criminals' vehicle and the registered address of the owner. Faces in the photographs were also matched against police records of suspected criminals. The gang was apprehended when their truck was surrounded and all the suspects are in custody.* Well done!' A proud smile stretched across Mr Grey's face. 'You not only survived, you also helped the police catch the bad guys.'

Beck shrugged. 'There were just a few of them. The whole illegal logging industry is way bigger. We didn't make much difference really.'

'Don't do yourself down,' Mrs Grey scolded. 'No one expects you to save the world on your own, Beck. But if everyone does just a bit – and you guys here have done way beyond that already – the world gets saved in the process. Right?'

The boys looked at each other and grinned.

* * *

They had spent a night with the police chief in the fishing village, then a jeep had come from Medan to collect them. Back at the hotel it had been hugs, tears and kisses from Peter's mum, while his dad tried to clear a path through the lobby. Beck had the impression he might have been in the doghouse for letting the boys stay behind in the jungle in the first place. But all seemed forgotten and the reunion was emotional and joyous.

Peter had grinned down at Hannah in her baby chair. 'You didn't even notice I'd gone, did you?'

Hannah had stared up at her brother as if it was the first time she'd ever seen a human. Then she abruptly lost interest and went back to trying to put her toe in her mouth.

But now that everyone was safe and the drama was over, there was no reason why they couldn't get on with actually enjoying the holiday. They had a fortnight booked, so they were going to use it. And use it they did. Beck finally got what he had been looking forward to on the first day – a regular family holiday. A bit of sightseeing. A bit of scuba diving. A bit of windsurfing. They bathed in hot springs where the steaming water was warmed by volcanic action. They sunbathed and splashed about in the hotel pool. But above all, they ate and drank until they were fit to burst.

Cool, fresh water had never tasted so good, Peter kept repeating, and every day Beck put extra croissants in his pockets at breakfast for later. 'Just in case!' he said with a smile.

It was the perfect antidote to all their jungle adventures.

And now it was their last day. In an hour's time they would be in a taxi heading for the airport.

* * *

The plane trundled to a stop at the end of the runway, then started to turn. Out of the window Beck caught a glimpse of the long stretch of tarmac, swinging round as the plane aligned with it. Then the engine sound rose to a roar, the seat pressed into his back and the plane moved forward to take off.

'You're doing it again,' Peter said as the plane tilted up. Beck had been fingering his neck thoughtfully. It always felt odd without his fire steel dangling there. The airline crews had a bit of a thing about passengers taking fire-making equipment on board. Whenever he flew he had to put the fire steel with his main luggage in the hold.

Sumatra fell away beneath them. The suburbs of Medan turned into small, tightly packed squares. The ground around the city was flat and green with paddy fields. And then the plane banked and turned over the jungle. Beck looked down at the canopy – the rises, the falls, the wisps of steam, all the way to the horizon – with wary respect. He couldn't say he'd enjoyed the experience. But he couldn't say he hadn't enjoyed it either. He was just glad to be seeing the back of it – for the moment, anyway.

And then he thought of the one thing they would have liked to do. He and Peter would have liked to meet Nakula's family to pay their respects. But that had not been possible; it turned out he didn't have any family. They had met Nakula's fellow keepers and learned that the job was his life. Protecting the orang-utans, keeping the jungle safe and free from human greed – that was all Nakula had ever done.

Beck was consoled that they had achieved something the dead keeper would have approved of. Mrs Grey had been right. Maybe they couldn't bring all the illegal logging activity to its knees, but they had done what they could, and Nakula would be proud.

Over the noise of the engines, Beck reckoned he could hear the roar of a tiger, agreeing with him.

BEAR'S SURVIVAL TIPS

TRACKS AND TRACKING

Tracking an animal in the wild takes real skill. You need good observational techniques, but you also need to know something about the animal you're tracking: what its tracks look like and how to follow them, how the animal behaves in the wild, and finally how to stalk it so that you can get a good look at it in its natural habitat.

Most animals leave very distinctive tracks. Before you go out in the field, try and find out what animals you're likely to find in that particular environment and what their tracks look like. After all, there's not much point in trying to track grizzlies in England or red squirrels in the Arctic.

Eventually you'll build up your own library of tracks, but here are a few common ones to get you going.

Badger

Badger tracks are 5–8cm long. You are more likely to see claw marks on the fore paws than the back paws.

Red fox

Red fox tracks are about 5cm long. They are sometimes covered with fur, which may make them less easy to see in mud or snow.

Deer

Different varieties of deer have different footprints, but mostly they have two teardrop-shaped halves, made by their cloven hooves. They are normally 4–8cm long.

Wild boar

Wild boar tracks are normally 5–7cm long.

Beaver

A beaver's hind print is about 15cm long. Once hunted to extinction in the UK, they were reintroduced in 2005 – seeing one is a real treat.

Otter

Otter tracks can be found near waterways. In very soft ground you might see evidence of webbed feet.

Rabbit

Rabbit tracks are one of the easiest to identify because their hind paws leave a much deeper impression than their fore paws.

Squirrel

The rear paws of a squirrel resemble a human hand, having five digits that look like four fingers and a thumb. The front paw (shown) has only four digits.

Vole

Vole tracks are quite similar to squirrel tracks. They are low down  the food chain, so their presence often gives you a clue that there are other animals about.

Hare

Hares rest in the open air, so their tracks may lead you to an indentation in the ground – or form – showing you where they have been.

Hedgehog

People traditionally leave bread soaked in milk out to attract hedgehogs. Don't – they find it indigestible and it can kill them.

BEAR GRYLLS is one of the world's most well-known adventurers. After spending three years in the British Special Forces with 21 SAS he set off to explore the globe in search of even bigger challenges. He has climbed Mount Everest, crossed the Arctic in a small boat and explored deserts, jungles and swamps worldwide. His TV shows have been seen by more than 1.2 billion viewers in more than 150 countries. In 2009, Bear became Chief Scout to the Scouting Association. He lives in London on a barge and on a small island in Wales with his wife Shara and their three sons: Jesse, Marmaduke and Huckleberry.

Read on for a peek at the next breathtaking
MISSION SURVIVAL adventure,

CLAWS OF THE CROCODILE

Chapter 1

Beck Granger is off to Australia!

Beck Granger had typed those words with a song in his heart. Finally, a month into the longest and most boring summer holidays *ever*, something was going to happen.

That was before supper. Now he had come back upstairs and checked his laptop to see how many friends had noticed his new status. He smiled when he saw the first name in the list of comments.

Peter Grey – Awesome sauce! You kept that quiet. Wish I was going with you but parents would have a fit lol.

Peter was his oldest friend from school. Their last two holidays together had been eventful: during the first they had been forced to parachute out of a plane

287

into the middle of the Sahara, escaping from murderous diamond smugglers. On the next one, a volcanic eruption had left them stranded in the Indonesian jungle. Threatened by illegal loggers, tigers and crocodiles, they had finally made their way back to civilization.

Yes, Peter's parents would certainly think twice before letting their son go off with Beck again.

These had been quite normal holidays for Beck. Except for the people trying to kill him. That was a little more unusual.

Beck's earliest memories were of travelling with his parents – before they went missing. The reason was always the same: Beck's father had been Special Operations Director of an environmental organization called Green Force, which worked for change through direct action. Whether it was high-lighting the plight of an endangered species, or championing the cause of a native people, or encouraging sustainable development in an area where modern farming was wreaking havoc – Green Force were there at the front line.

The work had taken his parents around the world,

so Beck had found himself with remote tribes in the most extreme spots, from the poles to the equator. And for a white English boy he had proved unusually good at learning how to stay alive. After his parents had vanished, Beck had travelled with his Uncle Al instead.

Now he was in his early teens. When it came to school grades, he knew he would never be more than so-so. When it came to survival, he knew he was up there with the best; but always with more to learn – like how to put up with a long, tedious English summer at home.

He typed a quick reply to Peter. *Didn't know till just now. I'll get you a cuddly koala!*

It had seemed like a good idea to keep the summer break empty. He had enjoyed the rest at first. Spending every night in his own bed. Eating cooked food that you'd actually bought in a shop. No one trying to kill him. These were all things he had felt he needed more of.

But now, halfway through the summer, he was itching for some excitement. He had been spending too much time on PlaceSpace, where his friends shared their holiday plans; he had never imagined that he would be envious of anyone heading for a hotel in Spain.

He had realized how bad it was when he found himself typing out survival advice to Peter:

Look out for hypothermia. It's not just shivering. Your speech gets sluggish and you lose co-ordination . . .

Peter and his family were in a caravan park in Wales. Hypothermia, a fatal cooling of the body's core temperature, was not going to be a problem. *Beck* had the problem. He just wasn't used to being the one stuck at home.

But then Uncle Al had dropped his bombshell.

'How do you fancy a trip Down Under?' he had asked.

Beck had almost cheered. Almost. But one thing he had learned: always get all the facts. And so he had just glanced sideways at his uncle. 'Why . . . ?'

Al had smiled at the wary tone. There was always a reason when they went travelling. 'It won't be five-star, I'm afraid. We'll be staying on the Casuarina campus of the University of Charles Darwin. It's all academic stuff. But for you – well, there's beaches, there's the national park, there's sailing . . .'

Al did not have to sell the idea to Beck. Just getting out of the house was enough.

'And what are *you* doing?' Beck asked.

Al looked slightly embarrassed, but pleased at the same time. 'They want to award me an honorary doctorate for my work on the impact of the first Aboriginal people on the prehistoric Australian environment.'

'Cool!' Beck was impressed, and glad for his uncle.

Uncle Al – Professor Sir Alan Granger, to the outside world – had dedicated his life to environmental causes. Becoming Beck's guardian when Beck's parents went missing in an air crash hadn't slowed him down. It wasn't always easy; sometimes it was downright dangerous. Al had upset a lot of powerful people in his time, and Beck reckoned it was only right for his work to be recognized.

'Sure, let's go Down Under!'

It was all too complicated to explain on PlaceSpace. Beck would give Peter the full story the next time they saw each other. He ran his eyes down the list of comments to the next name. What he saw made him sit up.

Brihony Stewart – That's great news! We can catch up. Come and see us in Broome?

Brihony! He hadn't seen her in years – not since . . . well, not since the last trip to Australia. She had been pretty cool, but he still tried not to think much about that particular trip. He had had a great time – mostly. But he had gone out with two parents and come home an orphan.

As representatives of Green Force, Beck's parents had gone out to the Kimberley, the region at the top end of Western Australia, to help an Aboriginal tribe fight a legal case. Beck had been taken under the wing of the tribal elders – once they realized that this English kid really *did* want to learn from them. He had assimilated a huge amount about surviving in the Outback.

What had been the name of his teacher? Pen . . . Pan . . . Pindari, that was it. A tough old guy, really hard to please, so that when you *did* please him, you really felt it had been worth it. His name meant 'high rocks', and he really was as tough as the ancient, sun-baked rocks of the Kimberley. Beck wondered where he was now.

So, yes, a great time . . . up until the moment his parents' plane crashed and Beck's life changed for ever.

Beck called up Google Maps to look up Broome, and also Darwin, where he and Al were going. Darwin was in the Northern Territory, nowhere near the Kimberley.

If Australia was a clock, then Darwin was perched on the north coast at the twelve o'clock position. Broome was at about ten o'clock. It looked no distance at all, but Beck wasn't fooled. The thing he remembered most clearly about Australia was that it was *enormous*. You could drop several United Kingdoms into it and they would just rattle around.

He looked at the scale in the corner of the screen, and saw that there was a good 600 miles between the two places. That was as the crow flies – a very long-distance crow with extra fuel tanks added. Go by road and it was 1,000 miles or more. Australia was big.

So, nice as it would be, he had to accept that he might not be seeing Brihony on this trip. But he didn't want to be negative, and who knew?

So he typed:

Yeah that would be cool. I'll let Al know.

Chapter 2

Twenty-one hours after leaving London, Beck finally managed to get some sleep. After what seemed like five minutes, Al was nudging him out of it. He gestured at the window of the Airbus and spoke in a terrible Australian accent.

'Welcome back, mate! That's the Kimberley out there.'

Beck peered blearily out from a height of 30,000 feet. 'Wow . . .'

Australia just *went on and on*. The vast plains disappeared into the horizon. Dust from the dry, arid ground blended into the haze of the sky so that it was impossible to see the join. The continent seemed to stretch on out over the edge of the world.

He thought again of his last visit. His parents –

and Brihony's – had been helping an Aboriginal tribe called the Jungun to prepare a case to take to the Australian High Court. Two hundred years earlier, an English farmer had taken a liking to some land; he had put a fence around it and claimed it as his own. The Jungun had already been living there for thousands of years, but that was easily taken care of: the farmer had guns and dogs; the Jungun did not.

Two hundred years on, the descendants of those Jungun had sued the descendants of the farmer, claiming their land back.

Beck looked out at the landscape and wondered why anyone was fool enough to think they could own any of it.

He also thought of Brihony. Once again he reminded himself that he wasn't going to the Kimberley this time. He and Al were heading for Darwin. One of the many things Pindari, his Aboriginal mentor, had taught him was not to live in the past. Be in the present; look to the future.

So, here in the present, Beck merely said: 'Was that meant to sound like an Australian?'

'Wasn't it any good?'

'It was great – if all Australians sound like a middle-aged Englishman.'

'If you don't mind, I'm an *elderly* Englishman, and proud of it.'

Beck laughed, and then the captain announced their arrival at Darwin within the hour.

There seemed to be a universal law that said passport queues had to be long and slow and boring. It had been like that in every airport Beck had ever visited, and the one at Darwin International was no exception.

He had turned on his phone a little while ago, and left it to sort itself out with the Australian network. Now, as they slowly shuffled forward, he swiped the screen to unlock it, and casually checked his emails and messages.

The PlaceSpace app notified him of a private message. Brihony again, maybe? He gave the screen a tap.

Jim Rockslide . . .

Beck froze, staring at his phone. It couldn't be! That was impossible! Thoughts whirled around his head. How on earth did a message from Jim Rockslide—

'Beck . . . ?' Al said gently, and Beck realized the queue had moved forward a couple of metres without him noticing. He hurried forward, then looked back at the phone. Al asked if something was the matter, but he just shook his head.

The message read: *Jim Rockslide – Friday 31st. Broome. Follow the White Dragon.*

Jim Rockslide? But Jim Rockslide didn't exist!

Jim Rockslide was a made-up character. Beck's dad used to tell him adventure stories about Jim Rockslide, the Hero Geologist who fought Nazis and aliens and smugglers all across the globe.

Beck jabbed at the PROFILE button to find out more about the sender. The profile page was empty, with just the standard outline of a human head instead of a photo. And that made sense, because Beck knew full well that only two people in the whole world had ever heard of Jim. Beck's dad, and Beck himself.

So how was a character made up by a dead man sending messages via PlaceSpace to Beck's phone?

* * *

Beck was still in a daze when they finally passed through passport control. He barely noticed the wait at baggage reclaim or their emergence into the arrivals area. If Al noticed he wasn't saying anything, he probably put it down to jetlag.

Beck's thoughts whirled. He could only think of one way he might have received that message . . .

His father was still alive.

No, he told himself immediately, his father *couldn't* still be alive.

OK, his parents' bodies had never been found, but . . .

But if they *were* still alive, then they must have only *pretended* to be dead all these years. He couldn't think of a single good reason why they would do that. How cruel would that be? What kind of a trick was that to play on their only son?

No, his parents were dead. They *had* to be.

But Jim Rockslide was sending him messages.

Round and round his thoughts went, and eventually one simple certainty came out of it all. Whatever this was about, whoever was sending him those messages . . . Today was Tuesday the 28th.

He needed to be in Broome on Friday the 31st.

'Oh, good grief . . .'

It took Beck a moment to realize that his uncle had said something. Al had got out his tablet as the taxi threaded its way through the suburbs of Darwin on the short trip towards the university. He was checking his own emails. It had been dark by the time they left the airport, so apart from streetlights and the headlamps and red tail-lights of other cars, Beck wasn't seeing much more of Australia.

'What's the problem?' Beck asked.

There was no hiding Al's irritation. 'Some fool – no one you know, but he's a big name – has gone and published a book that contradicts all my research. It's all about the extinction of the megafauna . . . He's wrong, of course, but I'm going to have to completely revise my acceptance speech at the university . . .' He smiled apologetically. 'I'm not going to be great company for the next few days, I'm afraid.'

Beck had no idea what 'extinction of the mega-fauna' meant, and he didn't care. It was like a ray of sunshine into his plans.

He had already checked travel options on his phone. There was a Greyhound coach to Broome every morning. The journey took nearly twenty-four hours.

So he could have tomorrow, Wednesday, to unwind in Darwin. He could travel all day Thursday, and be in Broome by Friday morning. And it wouldn't be like he was travelling into the unknown, because Brihony lived in Broome.

'You know,' he said casually, in a way that immediately made Al alert and suspicious, 'there might be a way around that . . .'

MISSION SURVIVAL

GOLD OF THE GODS

Would you survive?

Beck Granger is lost in the jungle with no food,
no compass, and no hope of rescue.

But Beck is no ordinary teenager – he's
the world's youngest survival expert.
If anyone can make it out alive, he can.

MISSION SURVIVAL

WAY OF THE WOLF

Would you survive?

A fatal plane crash. A frozen wilderness.
The world's youngest survival expert
is in trouble again . . .

MISSION SURVIVAL

SANDS OF THE SCORPION

Would you survive?

Beck Granger is about to face his toughest survival
challenge yet – the Sahara Desert. Blistering sun
and no water for hundreds of miles . . .

Can he survive the heat and make it out alive?

MUD, SWEAT AND TEARS

This is the thrilling story of everyone's favourite
real-life action man – Bear Grylls.

Find out what it's like to take on mountaineering,
martial arts, parachuting, life in the SAS – and all
that nature can throw at you!